Forbidden Surrender

by

Priscilla West

Table of Contents

Chapter One

"Leaving already?"

I'd tried my best not to wake my roommate as I collected the pile of client documents laying on the hotel room table. Riley Hewitt was a heavy sleeper, especially when she'd been out drinking the night before, her favorite vacation pastime. So I was surprised when she popped her strawberry-blonde head out from beneath the covers. Apparently, I hadn't been quiet enough.

"Sorry I woke you. I have to meet Richard downstairs in a few minutes so I'm just packing up." I'd been poring over the client strategy the previous night with my supervisor, Richard Hamm, in his hotel room as if we hadn't already gone over it dozens of times this past week.

When I'd gotten back to my room, I went over the materials again, memorizing every detail, replaying in my mind the sequence of events that would lead to Richard and me landing this client for our company. This meeting was a huge deal for not only Waterbridge-Howser, but also for me. Prestigious wealth management firms weren't in the habit of letting analysts with only three years experience fly to Cape Town, South Africa to woo billion dollar clients. It was only through a series of fortunate events—a group of senior employees leaving to start their own firm, my recent promotion, and a chance encounter with one of the directors in the cafeteria—that I was in this position. To say this was big would be an understatement.

"No worries." She yawned and rubbed one sleepy eye while making a noise somewhere between a groan and a gurgle. "I wanted to get up anyway. Get some breakfast, catch some foreign television. It's not every day you get to see Big Bird speaking Afrikaans. You ready for your meeting?"

God, I hope so. I'd better be after all the practice and preparation. Thankfully the butterflies fluttering in my stomach did more to energize me than a cup of coffee ever could. "I think I'm ready. Besides, Richard's going to do most of the talking. He's got years of experience doing this. I'm just there for backup."

She flashed her winning smile. "And to be a pretty face. You'll do great, Miss Harvard grad."

I stuck out my tongue playfully. Riley was from Staten Island and went to NYU for college. Although we both ended up working in the finance world, Riley was a corporate tax accountant thanks to her parents' guidance, and often reminded me how her job was less exciting than mine. We'd gotten to know each other over the past two years, sharing an apartment in the financial district of Manhattan to offset the exorbitant rent. Despite our personality differences—me being relatively straight-laced and Riley being the weekend warrior—we were both single professionals in their mid-twenties, so naturally we bonded.

When I'd told her I was taking a business trip to Cape Town for a week, she insisted on using her vacation time to join me. I couldn't blame her. The prospect of tanning on beautiful beaches and scoping out an exotic locale sounded more appealing than staring at balance sheets. Plus, I knew I would have some free time and hanging out with her would be much more fun than by myself or, heaven forbid, with Richard.

I packed up the last of my files, zipped up my shoulder bag, and smoothed out my light blue blouse and black pencil skirt. The outfit had been painstakingly put together to blend professionalism and style. It was part of the strategy. "How do I look?"

"I'd trust you with my million dollars—if I had it."

"Hopefully bad boy billionaire Vincent Sorenson thinks the same way."

"I've seen you working nonstop for this meeting for a month now. You're more than ready, girl. Either way, we're going to have fun tonight. Don't forget about that."

Of course, a full afternoon and evening of adventure with Riley. I was looking forward to it. With a wave, I left the hotel room and took the elevator down to the lobby where I was supposed to meet Richard. As I stepped onto the marble tile, my heel making a clack, I checked my watch. 7:30 a.m. on the button. We'd agreed to meet an hour before the meeting, giving us plenty of time to walk the few blocks from the hotel to the client's office building and to go over any last minute details should they arise in our sleep. God knows I'd had dreams about this moment. Well, more like nightmares. And for some funny reason, all of them ended with me in my underwear.

I spotted Richard seated on the edge of a cozy lounge chair, his eyes glued to his Blackberry. He wore a slate-gray suit with a cerulean tie, giving him the look of a diligent twenty-eight-year-old. Only the few strands of gray hair would betray he was closer to forty.

"Morning," I greeted him.

"Have you eaten breakfast yet, Kristen?" His response didn't include prying his eyes away from his device. It wasn't an unusual occurrence and I didn't take offense to it as I usually would have. If Richard could be boiled down to one word, it would be "business." It was both his strength and flaw. In the six months I'd worked under him, the only way I was able to get his undivided attention was by saying something relevant to his career advancement. In this, he was like most of the people who worked at the firm.

"I had an orange juice and a granola bar. I could go for some coffee though."

"Let's get going then. We can stop for a cup." He gathered his briefcase and I followed him as he left the hotel.

As we stepped out from beneath the overhang of the valet area, the view of the ocean in the distance and a cool breeze helped calm my nerves. It was the middle of June and the weather was amazing. We continued a leisurely stroll through the heart of downtown Cape Town. We had only flown in the previous day and had been busy with prep work so I hadn't had time to soak in my surroundings. Tall corporate buildings piercing the sky, honking cars, an eclectic mix of people commuting to work, a McDonald's on seemingly every corner—in a lot of ways, it reminded me of Manhattan. Still, the mix of bright colors, unfamiliar languages, and relaxed demeanors gave this place its own charm.

Along the way, we paused for a cup of coffee and Richard took the opportunity to review our strategy.

"When we get inside the building, I want you to be all smiles, Kristen. I want to see your teeth at all times. I will be doing most of the talking, but you play an important role as well. Clients may have more money than some countries, but first and foremost, they're people. People are emotional. Men, in particular, are weak to feminine allure. You soften them up, and I mold them."

Sounds like my role could be replaced by a cardboard cut out with boobs. Great. Richard's back-handed compliment irritated me but I wasn't in a position to rock the boat. Although there were plenty of women in the finance world, the upper echelons were men's clubs with their own rules. I'd hope to see that change one day, but unfortunately office politics were never my strong suit. The hours I put into gathering research documents on Vincent Sorenson and making persuasive graphs were enough for me. I really wanted to do well at my job, so I'd have to trust in Richard's experience.

"Right. An emotion-driven approach." I used his own words to show I understood him.

He smiled. "I call it the Buddy System. In my experience, Vincent's a Type B. Hobbyist, passionate for recreational activities, doesn't really know how to run a company but got extremely lucky. A hands-off CEO who's unburdened by details but good at delegating responsibility to his VPs. The guy loves to jerk off and surf."

I had my doubts about his assessment, but I kept them to myself. Vincent had started off as an avid surfer and built a cheap waterproof camera that allowed him to film his accomplishments. It seemed the only thing novel about his product was the attachment that fixed the device to his surfboard. People began asking him to build them one and through word-of-mouth it took off. Seven years later, his company SandWorks had expanded into various businesses related to extreme sports—bungee jumping, skydiving, mountain climbing, you name it. But based on all the internet pictures of the guy with his shirt off and surfboard in hand, you'd think he was a full-time beach bum.

A bum with tattoos and chiseled abs.

Richard continued as we crossed the street. "These guys are fairly predictable. All the other wealth management firms vying for his money look exactly the same on paper. They're going to talk to him about alpha ratios, dividends, hedge funds, and it's all going to go over his head. We want our approach to stand out. Demonstrating your interest in what he's passionate about is going to win you half the battle. Watch, I bet he'll be in a t-shirt, shorts, and sandals when we meet him."

My sensitivity to incorrect initial assumptions kicked in but I wasn't going to argue with Richard. Our strategy was set. Fortunately, Richard's confidence helped quell the gnawing feeling in my stomach that we were still unprepared. It was like the test anxiety I would get all throughout college except now failure meant losing millions of dollars instead of a few GPA points.

When we reached our destination, I faintly recognized the towering structure from our research. "Does Vincent own this building?"

"No. The company just rents out a few offices on the twenty-third floor for small operations in the area. He mainly comes here to surf."

I made sure to plaster my smile on before we passed through the revolving door entrance. After checking in, we took the elevator up to Vincent's floor where a receptionist ushered us to his office. "Just knock," she said before returning to her post.

"You ready?" Richard asked as he held his knuckle to the door.

This was it. I sucked in a deep breath and looked him in the eye. "Let's do this."

He knocked and I heard a distinctly male voice telling us to come in. Raising the corners of my lips to give my smile that extra perk, I followed as Richard led us in. My smile faded at the sight of the man seated behind the desk.

He was calmly poised with masculine refinement more befitting a Calvin Klein model than a Fortune 500 CEO. As I gazed at those rich brown eyes, sharply etched nose, and seductively carved mouth set in a bone structure undoubtedly designed by a master artisan I briefly thought we had stepped onto the set of a photoshoot. But there was no mistaking this was Vincent Sorenson, in the flesh. The hours I'd spent analyzing his images in the name of research did not—*could not*—prepare me for the real thing. In the most recent photo I could find, he was up to his waist in the sea and approaching the shore beaming a heart-stopping smile like some sort of mythical sex god eager to claim his offerings. It wasn't difficult to imagine virgins voluntarily sacrificing themselves to him.

But that picture was taken months ago and his dirty-blonde hair had been short then. Now it flowed, framing his features like a portrait fit for display in a museum. For an instant all I could think about was how it would feel to run my hands through those silky locks.

My footsteps slowed, matching my breaths as I watched him elegantly rise and circle his large oak desk, closing the space between us with economical finesse. After shaking Richard's hand, he stood in front of me. With brows furrowed in deep curiosity, his gorgeous eyes bored into my own, shrewdly assessing and evaluating. I felt strangely vulnerable and exposed under the weight of that stare, like I was undressed and naked before him.

I caught a whiff of something that made my mouth water and the area between my thighs ache. What was it? Cologne, after shave, his pheromones? Whatever it was, it smelled *good.*

Being so close, the raw magnetism he exuded jumbled my senses and made my pulse erratic. I felt compelled and pushed all at once; it was a potent male force that could never be bottled or captured on film, only experienced.

The sound of Richard's cough and subsequent nudge on my arm broke the spell.

My lips were dry so I licked them before speaking. "Hello Mr. Sorenson. Kristen Daley. It's a pleasure to meet you," I said evenly.

I held out my hand, feeling like the appendage didn't belong to me. I watched him take it with his own and squeeze firmly. The sensation alone was enough to summon pornographic images I neither approved of nor realized existed within me, ones where I was bent over his desk or splayed against a wall or on my knees. . .

"Vincent," he said, the velvety rasp of his voice flowing over me. The way he spoke his own name made it seem even more divine. "The pleasure's mine."

The heat radiating from his hand and up my arm seemed to reach my brain, and I forgot to squeeze back.

When he released his grip and shifted his gaze away from me, I was both relieved and disappointed to have the dirty mental images fade.

Pull yourself together. You're here for business.

"Great weather today," Richard remarked. "Perfect for surfing." He was already launching into the script.

It was then I noticed Vincent was wearing a t-shirt, shorts, and sandals—just as Richard predicted. The effect of the combination was more striking than I could have predicted and I figured he was the only man who could pull off sexy-casual well. Nevertheless, figuring the beach bum impression had been accurate, my fantasies subsided long enough to allow me to resume my feminine allure, smile included. It seemed to be working because I could feel Vincent's gaze slide over my profile as we moved to the meeting area of his office.

Vincent gestured and we took two accent chairs near the large glass wall facing the beach. It was a spacious office, bigger than any I had ever seen.

"I'd like to work on my cutback. I hear the Bali Bay is a great spot," Richard said. He had never surfed in his life.

Vincent sat across from us and I couldn't help studying him. Even in a position as benign as sitting, he exuded primal confidence. "It's one of my favorites." His deep voice resonated, inciting a restless energy in my legs. I shifted in my seat, trying to ignore the growing ache between my thighs. Fortunately, Richard was the one talking so Vincent's attention was trained on him.

Richard nodded enthusiastically. "From what I know, Kelly Slater got his chops riding those waves." This was part of the plan. Richard would open up with a softball about the weather then progressively use more surfing jargon, ultimately tying it back to investments through analogies. It was like a children's education program. I'd been skeptical—concerned the approach could be misconstrued as condescending—but when he spelled it out, the effective simplicity of the message was actually kind of brilliant.

Vincent's demeanor was impassive. "I see you've done your homework."

Receiving the anticipated signal, Richard continued, "The thing I admire most about him is his ability to read the water. They called him the Wave Whisperer."

We'd rehearsed the lines, me playing Vincent and Richard playing himself. It was standard best practice. Everything was going smoothly so far. Next, Vincent would say something along the lines of "I'm glad to hear you're a fan. Surfing's a big part of my company and you seem to understand that."

Vincent glanced at his expensive sea-diver watch. "I have another meeting soon, so if you don't mind, let's cut straight to the point. Why should I trust you with my money?"

Shit. This wasn't part of the plan. In a flash, I saw weeks of work flushed into oblivion. Panicking, I looked to Richard, hoping he'd pull something from a deep place of wisdom and experience.

Richard swallowed a hard lump, tiny beads of sweat dotting his brows. I'd never seen him so frazzled. "Of course, Mr. Sorenson. I'm going to let Kristen tell you more about our exciting investment strategies."

I reeled in horror when I realized where that deep place was.

My mouth opened to protest, but I quickly shut it to avoid ruining what remained of our facade of professionalism. I didn't dare look at Vincent, but I could feel his intense focus on me. Eyes wide, I fumbled through the documents in my dossier, trying my best to control my trembling fingers. If I screwed this up, Richard would blame me; he'd left me to drown.

"We've prepared materials illustrating the key benefits you'll receive from choosing Waterbridge-Howser," I somehow managed in a steady tone. I rose from my seat and walked over on shaky legs to hand Vincent the briefing materials we had planned to leave with him after we finished our pitch. What was I doing? Where was I taking this?

Stressed out by the situation as it was, I made an effort to avoid touching him in the exchange, but juggling the maneuver with everything else proved to be too complicated. I wobbled on my heels and fell, winding up with my chest and palms flat against his shirt, papers strewn across his lap.

I distantly registered strong hands catching my waist and my nipples instinctively tightened at the sensation. Something strange beneath my fingers caught my attention. Hard. Round. Circular. What was it?

He has nipple rings.

Curiosity overriding logic, my fingers pinched one of the rings through his shirt. I'd never met a guy who had nipple piercings before. His dark eyes locked with mine and I could swear for an instant I saw a spark turn into a smoldering fire.

When the silence passing between us became deafening, I collected my bearings and apologized emphatically.

"Are you okay?" he asked, his voice having the same effect on my body it had earlier.

No, your chest is too firm and I can't focus. "I'm fine, thank you. Sorry for the clumsiness. As I was saying, we have experts specializing in diverse strategies to fit your goals. Think of us as partners. Our firm helps your firm grow." He eyed me curiously and I felt my cheeks grow hot with embarrassment at the poor choice of words. "I mean wealth. Helps your wealth grow."

Awkwardly, I returned to my seat. It was the longest five steps I'd ever taken. Vincent was silent, his attention focused on the materials. I couldn't guess what he was thinking, only that the dark look in his expression couldn't be good. I tried to fill the void by verbalizing what he was already reading and in the middle of my meandering explanation about discretionary allocations, he cut me off. "Who made these charts?"

We were already bombing this presentation and this was going to be the nail in the coffin. Poor presentation, poor graphs. Could it get any worse?

"Kristen did," Richard said, surprising me. I made a mental note to strangle him when this was over.

Vincent looked at me with what I could only guess was a mixture of approval and fascination; it made him even more attractive, as if everything else wasn't enough. "They're good," he said, flipping the page and moving on to study the next document.

At the first sign of positivity, Richard attempted to salvage our chances. He cleared his throat and over the next fifteen minutes made an eloquent speech about value-added returns ending full circle with the surfing analogies we'd practiced. Apparently I'd bought him enough time to reformulate our strategy.

Still, only a few slight nods hinted Vincent had actually been listening. Mostly, he was just reading the materials I gave him.

"Any questions, Mr. Sorenson?" Richard asked.

"No. That's all I need to know." Vincent's rise from his seat indicated our meeting was over and we followed. "Thank you, Kristen." He shook my hand first, then Richard's. "Thank you, Dick." Richard paused then reciprocated the handshake, seemingly ignoring the misnomer.

When we left Vincent's office, my shoulders slumped and my body felt numb. Even the lively South African air couldn't reinvigorate me. On the walk back to the hotel, I was tempted to call Richard out on his behavior during the meeting, particularly the part where he threw the entire burden on my shoulders when things started going sour. I studied his features, expecting to find him dejected since he had more to lose than me, but he looked surprisingly calm.

"We blew it, didn't we?" I said, more as a statement than a question.

"Huh? I don't know why you think that."

"He wasn't responding to the emotion-driven strategy like we practiced. He barely said a thing."

Richard waved his hand as if dispelling an odor. "These brooding billionaire types, they just want you to think they're dark and mysterious. It gets the ladies but it's all an act. Did you see the guy? I was spot-on about his clothing. And I'm certain we aced that meeting. Don't worry."

I groaned. "Sure."

"Besides, I think he was into you. That move where you tripped and groped his pecs was perfect. We couldn't have planned something better." Richard chuckled.

"Don't tell anyone that happened," I snapped. It was bad enough Richard knew about that mishap, but it'd be even worse if more people at the firm found out—there was no telling how they would interpret it. The office gossip would be trouble.

"Your secret's safe with me." His finger to his lips completed the mockery.

"What are you doing the rest of the day?" I asked, wanting nothing more than to change the subject before my irritation with him made me speak out of line.

"Oh not much. Try the local cuisine, check out babes at the beach while I catch up on some emails."

"Which beach?"

"Clifton."

I smiled at him. Riley and I were definitely not going to that one.

Chapter Two

When I got back to my hotel room Riley was curled up on the bed watching television. Richard had gone to his own room to do who knows what.

"So how did it go?" Riley paused after I shot her a miserable look. "I'm so sorry, Kris. You don't have to talk about it."

I kicked off my heels and let my hair down, anxious to get out of professional mode. "Richard seems to think we did well. Sometimes I feel like he's in his own world though. Vincent was definitely not going for our pitch. You could totally read it in his body language."

Riley's expression was sympathetic. Remote in her hand, she switched off the TV. "I'm sure you did your best. Maybe luck just wasn't on your side today."

"That's the thing. I couldn't even do my best. I messed up multiple times." My mind replayed the awkward moments from the meeting and I shuddered. I didn't have anyone to blame but myself, but in my current mood I was eager for a scapegoat. "If Vincent wasn't so damn gorgeous, things might've been different."

"Oh, do tell." Her voice increased a pitch.

I told her all about my blunders, and when I was done she smiled. "Well at least you *looked* professional."

"Thanks for the sympathy." I gave her a wry grin.

"You know I'm always here for support. That's why we're going to have a blast today. You're going to forget all about that meeting and Mr. Abs Sorenson. Tonight we'll hit the bars and have guys buy us drinks. I know you haven't been dating much, all that sexual frustration must be eating you alive."

It was true. I'd only gone on a handful of unsuccessful dates since I'd met Riley. I told myself it was because I focusing on my career instead, but there were also personal reasons I didn't want to think about dating—reasons I never told Riley. Still, she was right about the sexual frustration. If my battery-operated boyfriend could talk, he'd probably say I was smothering him.

"I'm not really interested in the male species right now. Between Richard's chauvinism and Vincent shooting us down today, I think I'm a little burned out on testosterone."

"Fair enough. It'll just be us girls then. Get in that sexy bathing suit you brought." Riley untied her robe to reveal her bikini, its thin straps and enhanced bust leaving little to the imagination. "I'm all ready to go."

Having vented to Riley, I felt better about the situation this morning. I slipped into my bathing suit and left the hotel with her.

When we arrived at the aptly-named Bikini Beach just before noon, the shore was packed. There was a nice mix of tourists and locals, with lots of people both in and out of the clear blue waters. We laid our towels down on the heated sand and relaxed in cheap folding chairs we got from a nearby beach store. Once we were settled, Riley went to get us some drinks. I stared out at the waves and thought about how picturesque the scene looked. This kind of experience was rare when you lived in Manhattan and I took the opportunity to soak it in. As the afternoon wore on, the stress of the morning seemed to melt away like the ice cubes in our mojitos.

I spotted a few surfers in the distance zig-zagging along the water. I'd never been surfing before and didn't have much of a desire to change that. I understood the appeal, but I was afraid of the danger—I just didn't think the risks outweighed the benefits. A few thrilling moments versus the possibility of getting my arm bitten off by a shark or getting stung by a jellyfish . . . yeah, I'd be happy with just tanning—with sunscreen of course.

Vincent, on the other hand, loved risky activities. His whole business was based on extreme sports. I didn't really get it but it clearly made him very successful.

A few toned men with olive skin passed by and Riley directed my attention to them. I had to admit they were attractive from a purely physical perspective but that just didn't do it for me.

"Maybe your standards are too high," Riley said.

"Just because they have abs and a penis doesn't mean I want to sleep with them."

She laughed. "Keith had more than that. You never told me why you turned down my offer to set you up with him."

"He just wasn't my type."

"What *is* your type, Kris? I've hardly seen you date since I've known you, and don't say it's because you've been too busy with work." She nudged me with her elbow.

"I'm not sure I have one." I was only vaguely aware of rubbing my own pinky finger.

"Oh come on. Every girl has a type, some just aren't willing to be honest about it."

Now I was the curious one. "What's your type then?"

"Let's see . . . tall, strong, handsome, smart, dark, dangerous . . . oh and let's not forget rich."

"Sounds more like a fantasy than a real person." Actually that sounded a lot like someone I met this morning. "Why don't we just say I like the 'nice and caring' type."

"Basically boring then, huh?"

"Boring to you, satisfying to me. Why would you want someone dark and dangerous? And if he's so hot, wouldn't you be concerned he'd cheat on you?"

"I'd just have to blow his mind." Her mischievous wink made it clear what she meant. "But to each her own."

We spent the rest of the afternoon bathing our skin in UV rays and trying out the local food. Fortunately, there were enough tourists streaming through Cape Town that the restaurants provided menus in English. I thought chicken would taste the same no matter where you were but whatever special sauce they used made it exceptionally delicious. We explored the area, stopping periodically to point out unique architecture or unusual occurrences. Although I'd told Riley I wasn't interested in dating, I couldn't help but indulge in idle thoughts about

Vincent. Maybe I'd spent way too much time memorizing his files.

It was evening by the time we were hungry again. Despite wearing comfy sneakers, our feet were killing us from all the walking. Riley suggested we rest at a local bar to relieve our weary legs and grab some grub. We were off the beaten path by this point and the bar she picked looked sketchy.

"It'll be fun. Don't you want to get an authentic experience? We didn't fly thousands of miles just to go to some bar we could go to back home."

"Yeah, but we're two American girls in a foreign country. There are horror movies based on this situation."

"What's the worst that can happen?" Her grin made me ill at ease.

"Don't say that."

"Look, I have some mace in my bag. If anybody tries to get frisky with us, I'm going to melt their eyeballs." I pictured Riley as the female version of Rambo.

"All right, fine. If we get abducted, it's your fault. I just don't want you saying I'm a party pooper."

She laughed. "I've never said that. You just like to be cautious, which I respect. Remember when you warned me about Danny? You were right, he did turn out to be a creep."

Riley had dated Danny a few months prior. When she brought him over to our apartment he kept giving me shifty-eyed stares. I expressed my concerns to her and it turned out he had done time in prison for theft. He wasn't even the worst of Riley's extensive dating history. I honestly didn't know how she found some of these guys.

Upon entering, we found the place was full of mostly locals. There were a few expats in the corner who sounded British and were probably out for some adventure. Somewhere there was a speaker putting out exotic tribal music. The hypnotic beats were catchy but it certainly was a far cry from American pop music—no Miley Cyrus here. When we found a seat at a table and ordered margaritas, I found myself easing into the atmosphere.

"Man, check this place out." Riley sounded excited. She pointed at the decorations around us. "Animal bones hanging on the walls, a shrunken head behind the bar, and a beat-up sign that says 'Ompad'. Isn't it cool?" She whipped out her phone to snap some pictures.

The distinct sound of a shot glass slamming against wood alerted us to a commotion brewing near the bar. A group of onlookers surrounded two men with tumblers in hand and a bottle half-full of amber liquid between them. The one on the left was a juggernaut of a man; a gruff beard and mean stare completed the intimidation factor. The gathering of curious spectators obscured my view of the man on the right.

"What's going on over there?" Riley asked.

I knew we shouldn't have gotten closer. The feeling in my gut that whatever was going on over there was trouble told me we should leave, but intense curiosity pulled us near the action like moths to a flame.

We settled at a table nearby, giving us front row seats. It was when I saw who the figure poised on the right was that I realized why my alarm bells had gone off.

Vincent.

What was he doing here? He was wearing a white button-down and khakis that showcased his lean muscular build. By now the crowd around the bar had grown considerably, tantamount with the noise level. Most huddled around Vincent's side. Some of the admirers included beautiful, curvaceous women that were all but rubbing their breasts against Vincent, and a pang of jealousy hit me from who knows where.

Riley shouted to me over the ruckus. "Is that who I think it is?"

"Yeah, it's Vincent," I said. "Looks like he's in the middle of some kind of drinking game."

I couldn't hear her response over the cheering. The only two words I managed to decipher were "fucking" and "hot."

I leaned in closer to her. "I can't hear you."

"I said you should go over there. This could be your second chance to win him over."

"What? I don't even know what he's doing. He might not even remember me."

"You pinched his goddamn nipple, of course he'll remember you. Go find out." She nudged my shoulder but I remained steadfast in my seat. As serendipitous as this encounter was, I wasn't comfortable with the idea of approaching Vincent in this strange social situation. If Richard had been right about the meeting going well, talking to Vincent could sabotage our efforts rather than help.

"Let's just watch them a little first."

We witnessed the burly guy down his shot, slam his glass against the counter, and grunt something in Afrikaans. I couldn't understand it, but if I had to guess by the tone, it meant "Is that the best you got?" He then reached into a nearby bag sitting on the counter and produced a large clear jar. I squinted my eyes to identify the contents. Thin strands, black dots scurrying.

Cobwebs and spiders.

The crowd didn't seem surprised, instead they clamored approval like they were at a sporting event. Why would he have such a thing? And here of all places. *I hate spiders.*

My disgust and surprise must have been palpable because Vincent turned his head in my direction as if attuned to my specific frequency. For the second time today, we locked eyes. A part of me wanted to hide from the embarrassment of this morning, another part of me knew my company had important business to conduct with him.

Before I decided whether I was going to wave at him or shrink behind the crowd of bodies, a ghost of a smile touched his lips.

He waved me over. In disbelief, I pointed my finger at my chest as I mouthed "me?" and he nodded. What did he want with me? I looked to Riley for advice and was met with eager shooing motions. Sensing an opportunity to clear up any confusion over this morning's meeting, I worked my way through the crowd to him. The women around him were reluctant to make room, shooting me catty-glares, but I managed to wiggle through an opening.

"Hello Kristen," he said.

He did remember my name. "Hello Mr. Sorenson."

"Please, just call me Vincent. I didn't expect to see you here, but now that you are, this'll be a lot more interesting." He grinned.

I wasn't sure what he meant. Confused by the whole situation, I asked, "What are you doing here, Vincent?"

"Business. And you're going to decide if you want to help me." He gestured to the big guy and his bizarre pet spiders.

Okay . . . that doesn't explain a whole lot.

"I should tell you, Mr. Sorenson. I have a fear of spiders," I said, eyeing the jar.

He leaned close to my ear so I could hear him. "All the better. You asked for my money earlier today, Kristen." His smoky voice was implacable. "I wasn't impressed. Here's your second chance to convince me to trust you with my assets."

Shit. We *did* blow the meeting this morning. I gulped. "What do you want me to do?"

As if to answer my question, the hulk uncapped the jar and picked out a spider with a pair of chopsticks.

The sight of the tiny black creature outside its confines made me panic. I tried to escape but Vincent caught my elbow in a light but secure grip and pulled me to him. "You're fine, trust me. Just watch."

With his hand on the filled shot glass, the big guy placed the spider on the skin between his thumb and forefinger. The spider—whose backside displayed a red dot— remained surprisingly still, perhaps in as much suspense as I was. Never taking his eyes off the poisonous creature, the big guy slowly brought the drink to his lips, keeping his hand steady, and in one smooth motion downed the contents, flicked the spider off his hand, and crushed the arachnid as he slammed his glass on the bar. The crowd erupted in cheers.

The big guy looked expectantly at me and Vincent. His steely eyes said "your turn".

"You're not seriously going to do that are you?" I blurted without thinking.

His eyes narrowed as he smiled. "I am. And you're going to help me by putting the spider on my hand."

I was about to say "hell no" but thought better when I noticed his probing eyes. "I'm really not comfortable with this."

"Consider it a test. How far are you willing to go to serve my interests?"

I felt my breaths shorten. "Are we talking about money here or poisonous spiders? Because those are two very different things."

"Believe it or not, there's a lot at stake if I don't follow through." He gestured to a pile of documents on the counter. I couldn't read the language, but from the formatting I could tell they were contract documents—so this wasn't just a wager between two inflated egos. "I imagine there's also a lot at stake for you."

"What if it bites you?"

"Let me worry about that. If it does, it won't be your fault."

"What if it climbs up and bites me?"

"I won't let it happen. Trust me, you'll be fine."

This wasn't professional; this was insane. Crazy. I'd never done anything close to this dangerous before. If I had known I'd have to handle deadly bugs to win clients, I might not have taken this job in the first place.

I was stuck between a rock and a hard place: don't do it and for sure lose Vincent as a client; do it and possibly kill both the hottest man I'd ever met and my career. Either way, I was screwed.

I glanced over at Riley and saw her give me a thumbs up.

Damn you, Vincent. I picked up the chopsticks and unscrewed the jar, grimacing as I lowered the utensil inside. When I touched one of the creatures, it moved and I instinctively retracted my hand.

"No way. I can't do this," I exclaimed.

"Giving up so soon? Nothing worth pursuing comes without risk."

Inflamed by his taunting, I tried again. This time the black creature didn't move and I was able to clamp it with the chopsticks. It felt hard and squishy at the same time and when I pulled it out and got a better view of its wriggling legs, it took every ounce of willpower not to throw it across the bar. My hands were trembling and I was afraid I'd drop the spider or worse, rile it up enough to bite Vincent. Then a warm hand around my upper arm steadied me.

"You're doing great. Just relax a little. Focus on controlling your own body, not on what you're holding."

"Easier said than done," I replied, even though his advice seemed to be working.

The next few moments were a blur, but I somehow managed to place the spider gently on Vincent's hand. He downed his drink and went the extra mile by flicking the spider back into the jar instead of killing it.

Once again, the bar roared approval.

Afraid I would have to do it again, I turned to the big guy and was relieved to see him passed out on the counter.

Vincent had won.

Chapter Three

It wasn't long before the ruckus died down. The big guy had woken up, signed the contract, shook Vincent's hand, and left. The crowd had dissipated and Riley was now being entertained by one of the British guys from the expat group. I found myself seated beside Vincent at a cozy table in a secluded part of the bar, alone.

Even with all the alcohol I imagined was flowing through his system, Vincent looked as sober as a judge. Not only were his nerves steel, but so was his blood. I began to wonder if those were the only parts . . .

"What can I get you to drink?" Vincent asked, flagging the waitress.

I considered avoiding more alcohol in case we discussed business, but I didn't want to be rude either. "A mojito please."

The waitress flashed a flirty smile at Vincent before leaving, which made me bristle.

He returned his attention back to me. "I'm surprised. You struck me as more damsel than dame."

The comment was decidedly personal and I felt justified in taking offense. "And you strike me as more reckless than brave. Why were you in a drinking contest with a spider-loving thug?"

His sinful lips curved into a wicked smile. "You can't always judge people by their appearance. Nambe is a real estate mogul. He owns a lot of property in the area including this bar. I wanted one of his private beaches and he set the terms. You'll find the most successful people play by their own rules."

His comment made me recall how far I had just gone to win him over as a client. "Do all your business transactions involve endangering your life?"

"Just the interesting ones. The bite wouldn't have been fatal if I went to the hospital immediately. When you want something bad enough, sometimes it's surprising what you're willing to do." He adjusted his seat and his leg brushed mine sending an unwelcome flutter through my belly.

The waitress returned with my drink and I took a sip, relishing the taste more than I should have. "Does that apply to swimming with sharks and jumping off cliffs?" I said, feeling emboldened by the mojito as well as the other alcoholic beverages I'd consumed since setting foot inside this bar.

"It applies to whatever gives me a thrill. What gives you a thrill Kristen? Besides winning my account."

Unsure if that was a flirtatious line or an accusation, I answered, "Who says that gives me a thrill?"

"It makes you good at your job. Pitch aside, the materials you gave me were polished."

"Thank you." I flustered at the compliment. It was rare to have my work given the appreciation I felt it deserved even by my colleagues, let alone a client.

"What would you do if I chose your company?"

"You're saying after I did all that, you're still not convinced you can trust us with your money?"

"What you did puts Waterbridge-Howser back in the running. After your partner insulted my intelligence this morning I had almost ruled you out."

Crap. "I'm truly sorry about that, it wasn't intentional. We were just trying to be persuasive and it seems we missed the mark."

"Fair enough." He stirred his drink and shrugged. "I'm curious, what are you doing in a bar like this?"

The question sounded like he thought I was here on the prowl—which was not at all the reason. "It was my friend Riley's idea." I pointed a blaming finger at Riley across the bar, who seemed to be too enamored with her company to notice. "She's a little adventurous."

"So are you," he said touching my hand with the tip of his finger. "Do you have a boyfriend?"

"Excuse me?" The conversation had turned decidedly flirtatious and I wasn't sure how to react. I'd never been hit on by a potential client before and there were no company guidelines addressing this type of situation. Regardless of how attracted I was to Vincent, if anybody at work suspected I was mixing business with pleasure, my professional reputation would be ruined. I'd seen it happen before.

"Don't tell me your partner is."

"You mean Richard? He's definitely *not* my boyfriend."

"Good. So you're single." He leaned his breathtaking face closer to mine heightening awareness of him.

I stood my ground. "Maybe I am, maybe I'm not. Either way I'm sorry to disappoint you, but I don't date potential clients," I said, hoping the brush-off would end the personal discussion and we could return to talking about business.

Those seductive lips so close to mine curved into a smile. "Who says anything about dating? I just want to finish what you started this morning."

"What are you talking about?"

"We were here." He gently but firmly took my hand in his and placed it on his chest. The move caught me off guard and all I could do was suck in a deep breath when I felt the sudden warmth of his body and the strong beat of his heart beneath my palms. "Let's move it further." He began to move my hand slowly downward. As my fingertips traced the hard contours at the base of his pecs and the firm cut of his stomach through his shirt, goosebumps ran across my skin and the hairs on the back of my neck stiffened. My pulse quickened and my lips parted to accommodate faster breaths. It wasn't until my fingers reached the base of his stony abs that my mind caught up and I pulled away.

"This morning was an innocent mistake," I shot back, aware I was more aroused than offended by the gesture. "I don't know what kind of girl you think I am exactly, but I don't mix business with pleasure."

"I do." His sexy voice could tear down any woman's defenses. I knew I had to get away, afraid I wouldn't be an exception.

"Good for you. Thank you for the drink Mr. Sorenson but if you'll excuse me, I need to get back to my friend." I rose from my seat with the intention of leaving but turned back to that gorgeous face one last time. "If you're still interested in Waterbridge-Howser, you have Richard's number."

His lips curled into that same wicked smile from earlier. "We'll be in touch."

When I returned to Riley's table, she was by herself.

"What happened to the British guy?" I asked.

"I got bored with him. But nevermind that. What happened with you and you know who?"

"Nothing. It was just a professional discussion. All business." I was trying to convince myself as much as her.

"Yeah, right. You're going to get laid tonight."

I shook my head vehemently. "No," I repeated. "Let's go. I've had enough of this place."

Chapter Four

We had taken off two hours ago from Cape Town International and were heading back to JFK. Riley and I had made the most out of the rest of our stay; we hadn't had fun like that in a long time and I was already dreading returning to work. While I enjoyed working at Waterbridge-Howser, no job beat out long scenic hikes around Cape Town and watching Riley flirt with the locals.

I looked over to see Riley still fast asleep next to me, her head lolling on the backrest. If only I could get a few minutes of shuteye. Riley had tried to prod me about what happened between Vincent and me at the bar, but I left it vague, knowing that she would never let it drop if she knew the truth.

My head still pounded from the celebratory shots she insisted we take for our last "night" in South Africa. She had made some new friends on the beach who took us to the best viewing spot in town, and we'd stayed up all night watching the sun rise over Table Mountain. I had to admit, it was gorgeous, but we regretted it afterwards when we had to pack and head to the airport. Bleary eyed with the beginnings of what I was sure would be an awful hangover, we dragged ourselves to the gate and boarded. Riley had fallen asleep almost as soon as she sat down.

The ding of the seatbelt sign brought my attention back to the folder open in front of me. Richard had sent me an email late the previous night asking me to look over Vincent's file again. He was nervous that Vincent hadn't called us yet, which made me nervous as well.

We hadn't seen any sign of Vincent Sorenson after that night at the bar. When we were exploring the wilderness around Cape Town, I was half expecting him to pop out of a forested area nearby locked in a mortal engagement with a panther, or make a dramatic appearance by falling out of the sky with a parachute. Something death defying. But there was nothing.

That night, Vincent had been so close to me I could smell the masculine scent of whiskey and spice from his clothes. I remembered his mouth lingering close to mine as he trailed my fingers down the chiseled expanse of his torso. I wondered how his lips would feel against my exposed neck. Would his kisses be soft or desperate?

I shook the thought out of my head as I flipped through Vincent's file. He had studied mechanical engineering at Berkeley, though his professors would have said he had majored in surfing, and mechanical engineering was just his pastime. He graduated and promptly took up a life of surfing and seasonal jobs. But a few years later, he designed and built the first prototype of his surfboard camera by himself in his apartment—he seemed like he knew how to use his hands and was obviously into mixing business with the rest of his life.

I recalled the texture of his hands from when he pulled my hand to his chest at the bar. They were neatly maintained but strong and calloused from all his outdoor activities. A slow heat gathered in my core as I imagined him sliding them up my thighs—I had resisted him in Cape Town but I wasn't sure I could resist his intimate touch again.

I shook my head. One encounter with Vincent Sorenson and I was already squirming in my panties. Since when did I start fantasizing about near strangers, and potential clients at that? Besides, anything happening between me and Vincent was bound to be a dead end. Those women around him at the bar were a thread away from having their dresses pooled on the floor. How could I compete with that? Did I even want to? I'd made a mistake with a man like that once, but I wasn't about to do it again.

Riley let out a soft snore, her head rolled with the tilting of the plane and stopped gently on my shoulder. She always made it seem so easy. If she wanted a guy, nine times out of ten, she got him. What would she have done with Vincent? I shook away the thought.

Whatever reason Vincent Sorenson had for not contacting us, I just hoped it didn't have to do with me shooting down his advances. I put the papers carefully back into the folder and tucked them away. Vincent was only a dangerous fantasy that needed to disappear. I leaned my head back and pulled the itchy airline blanket over my head, hoping to get some sleep before we arrived in New York.

***

My legs were rubber and sweat drenched the shirt on my back. I was willing my legs to move but they wouldn't. The air was the consistency of mud. What was I running from?

Run. Just run.

Fear coiled in the pit of my stomach and I wanted to vomit.

Someone was behind me. Blue eyes burning hot and cold at the same time behind thick spectacles. How can he be so fast? He grabbed my arm, twisting it behind me. Pain flashed through my shoulder, but I couldn't open my mouth to scream.

The shrieking of my alarm clock woke me up. I ripped my sheets off, damp with sweat. Damn it, I'd thought I was over that. I shook my numb right arm, aware I must've been sleeping on it all night, and clumsily hit my hand against the nightstand in confusion before I realized the alarm clock had fallen on the floor. Reaching down, I picked it up and squinted at the red letters. 7:00 a.m. I got up and snuck into the bathroom, noting Riley's bedroom door was still closed. She didn't have to get to work until nine, and she usually slept in until the absolute last minute.

My heart rate had slowed to normal by the time I finished my morning shower and dressed myself for work. I took the elevator down, sipping on my breakfast smoothie. Broccoli, oatmeal, protein powder, orange juice, a banana and yogurt: it was the breakfast of champions. Riley introduced me to it as a hangover cure, but it quickly became my go to morning snack. Looking at my reflection in the elevator doors, I decided I'd definitely dressed the part of a professional in my white blouse, a-line skirt, and black heels. Heck, if I had a few million dollars I'd trust myself with the money.

I power walked the streets of the Lower West side until I reached the subway station, only slowing to step over the manhole covers to avoid getting my heels stuck. At the intersection, a herd of commuters merged with me. Men and women in business suits moved in perfect synchronicity, all without any conversation.

That was the strangest thing about New York City I had never gotten used to. People could be right on top of one another but no one ever said a word. It was similar in Boston where I went to college and worked for a year afterward, but before that I lived in Coppell, Texas, where nearly everyone knew your name. You just felt more like a person when people actually recognized your existence.

I still thought of Texas as home, even though I hadn't been back in years. My parents still lived there but we'd been out of touch since I left for college. They were workaholics and expected the same of me—at the expense of my childhood and a real relationship with them. I wasn't bitter, but I also wasn't fond of their attempts to steer my life. They had their own lives now and I had mine.

The waves of commuters swept me along with them into the Bowling Green Station. I supposed ignoring strangers was a coping mechanism when you lived in a city of eight million. You couldn't learn the names of everyone even if you wanted to.

Twenty minutes later, I stepped out of the elevator on the forty-eighth floor of the gleaming steel and glass structure that was home to Waterbridge-Howser. A marble accented mahogany reception desk greeted me. Aluminum letters spelling out the company's name hung tastefully on the wall behind the desk. The conference room to the right was empty, the view of the park filtering through it. Every detail was designed to demonstrate wealth and power. Appearances were important in this business.

I navigated through the cubicle maze to my desk. We weren't packed together as tightly as possible, but it wasn't the open office plan of a design studio either. Tall dividers gave analysts their privacy as they investigated investment opportunities. Some analysts, like myself, were experienced enough to talk to clients directly, answering their questions and handling minor issues so the higher-ups would be free to work on bringing in more business. The managers' offices formed the perimeter of every floor, each one with a window view. The partners of the firm had their own section of the floor, and they only ever emerged to speak to the managers.

I dropped my satchel onto my desk and pulled out Vincent's file before heading through the outer rim of the cubicle corral to Richard's office. His door was half open and he was typing something on his computer.

"Richard, you wanted to meet about Mr. Sorenson?"

"Yes. Come in. Did you look over his file?" he said, not looking away from his screen.

"I checked everything and even reviewed our proposal. Our suggestions were very reasonable based on what we know about his finances."

Richard looked directly at me. "Any idea why he hasn't called us yet?"

In a second of irrationality, I thought about blurting out the details of meeting Vincent at the bar but decided it better if Richard didn't know anything about that. Besides, it was irrelevant. If anything, Vincent would have been more interested in working with us after that meeting.

I shrugged. "I don't know, maybe another firm got to him before us?" I remembered Richard's condescending comments about the "Wave Whisperer" and his assumptions about Vincent's lifestyle that no doubt influenced his approach to the meeting. That might have something to do with the fact that we hadn't heard from Vincent, but I kept my mouth shut.

Richard frowned. "Screw it. Nothing to do now but wait. Let me know if you hear anything."

I took the cue that the meeting was over when Richard turned back to his computer. When I got back to my own desk, I pulled up my email. The first thing that popped up was a message from my cell phone provider informing me I had reached my data limit for the month. *Again?* These cell phone services really knew how to fleece you. I deleted the email and moved on, reviewing work memos and deleting spam.

The rest of the morning bled into the afternoon. After eating lunch and helping another analyst resolve a reporting issue, I came back to my desk to find a note thrown haphazardly over my keyboard.

Kaufman called, have to meet him. Keep me updated if Sorenson calls the office.

Jon Kaufman was one of the larger clients Richard handled. He had a large plastics refinery west of the Hudson and was one of the clients who didn't come to our office. Rather, we went to him. I never met the guy but from the way Richard spoke about him, he was difficult.

I put the note aside and settled into my routine. I had barely gotten into the zone when my phone rang.

"Hey Kristen, I have Mr. Sorenson on the line for you." Our receptionist sounded like she was going to pass out just from the mention of his name.

So we hadn't blown our chances completely. For a moment I considered the possibility Richard had been right. *These guys are fairly predictable.* But there was no way Richard gave Vincent a positive first impression, and if anything saved us, it was probably my stunt with the spider at the bar.

"Thanks, transfer him over." I kept my voice level despite being aware that Vincent had asked for me specifically. I'd told him to call Richard as part of my brush-off. I just hoped his intentions were business.

A beep later and Vincent's silky voice vibrated through my handset.

"Hello Kristen."

Even over the phone, his velvety rasp made it difficult to maintain my composure. I switched the phone to my left hand and wiped my sweaty palm on my skirt.

"Hello Vincent, it's good to hear from you," I said, feeling like I'd just swallowed a cotton ball.

"I've been thinking about our meeting."

Which meeting? The one where I played with his nipple ring or the one where he asked me to mix business with pleasure?

"I'd like to discuss business," he continued.

I exhaled, relieved he wasn't interested in revisiting our personal discussion. Maybe he took the hint. "I'm happy to hear that. When would you like to schedule a meeting?"

"Today."

I laughed nervously. "We might need a little more time to make it out to South Africa."

"I'm at my office in Manhattan. Sixty-five West Fifty-ninth Street. Eighty-second floor." That was just a few blocks away. Of course. He had a media office in Manhattan that produced a popular extreme sports series that were broadcast on multiple cable networks.

"Could we do tomorrow? Richard is meeting with another client until late this afternoon."

"He's not needed. I'll be on a flight to Lucerne tomorrow. It has to be today." His voice betrayed no sense of urgency or need, just a statement of facts.

My mind swirled. Could I take the meeting with Vincent? I had all the paperwork ready; it was in the same folder as the proposal. Richard had let me close some smaller clients before so I knew what had to be done. But what would he say if I went to the meeting without him? I had a pretty good guess of what he'd say if I was the reason we lost Vincent's business. I had to take this meeting, if only to avoid the four letter words Richard would have in store for me if I didn't.

"Yes, of course. How is three p.m. for you?" I asked.

"Perfect. I'm looking forward to it, Kristen."

After he hung up, I let out a long breath, blowing my bangs out of my face. I was going to see Vincent Sorenson again. Although I certainly hadn't forgotten about both our meetings in South Africa, I wasn't sure if he'd been thinking about them at all.

At two thirty, I quickly packed my bag and told the receptionist to tell Richard or anyone else who stopped by my desk that I was going to be at a client meeting.

It was only when I was on the elevator down, the paperwork neatly filed in my briefcase, that I realized what I'd gotten myself into. Vincent Sorenson and I were going to be in the same room together. Alone.

***

Well this is different.

I stood in front of the sleek black reception desk at Red Fusion, SandWork's media arm, trying not to eye the curved adult-sized plastic slide that came from the ceiling and ended just right of where the receptionist was sitting. I smiled at the blonde woman behind the desk. She beamed back at me. Her rows of perfectly white teeth and her sultry figure made her more appropriate for a movie set than an office.

"Can I help you?" she said.

"Hi, my name is Kristen Daley. I'm here to see Mr. Sorenson."

"Of course, he's expecting you. Right this way." I followed her, watching the way her hips swayed in her curve-hugging dress. Though I tried to resist, I couldn't help inspecting my reflection in the glass door to make a quick comparison. Was she one of the pleasures Vincent mixed with his business? But so what if she was? I had no right to be upset.

The Red Fusion offices were abuzz with activity. An employee sat cross-legged on the carpet, tossing a stress ball at the wall, stopping only to peck furiously at the laptop in front of him. Others were seated around large tables, having animated discussions. It was nothing like the reverential near silence at Waterbridge-Howser.

"Here we are, you can go inside. Vincent's ready for you." The receptionist stopped in front of a frosted glass door. The same glass formed a wall that stretched to either side of the entry.

I nodded thanks to her before pushing open the door and walking inside. Silence greeted me. Whatever the glass was made of, it completely blocked the noise from outside. In the corner was a black leather couch with a small coffee table in front of it. A large desk was set squarely in the center of the room, a metal and glass tribute to modernity. It was a stark contrast to his desk in Cape Town.

Vincent stood by the window, one arm behind his back, looking out. He was wearing a navy suit matched with a grey tie and white shirt. His long locks were slicked neatly back. Unwillingly preoccupied with wild fantasies, I nearly tripped on the rug in front of his desk as I walked closer. My pulse danced in my veins and a flush coursed through my cheeks. If I had fallen on him twice, I would've died from embarrassment.

Blue skies and skyscrapers along Central Park silhouetted his figure. He looked equally comfortable in a suit as he had in shorts and flip-flops.

He turned around, his dark eyes shimmering. "Beautiful, isn't it?"

I looked at his chin, chiseled with perfect angles, as if carved from a slab of marble. My eyes moved up to his mouth, his lips full and soft.

I cleared my throat. "Yes, it is. I've never quite gotten used to the view. Good to see you again, Mr. Sorenson."

"Please Kristen, have a seat." I stumbled to the guest chair in front of his desk while Vincent remained by the window.

I took it as my cue to continue. I set my bag down and reached inside for the glossy documents Richard and I prepared for a follow-up meeting.

Vincent studied me for a moment, his head tilted slightly to one side, as if examining a piece of art. Or his prey. Not knowing what else to do, I unleashed my rehearsed speech. "Thank you for meeting with me again. Waterbridge-Howser will be an excellent choice for your wealth management needs. We offer personal attention as well as products that larger—"

He held his hand up to stop me. "I've decided to go with Waterbridge-Howser." He glided from the window to me, occupying the small space between my seat and his enormous desk. He leaned back and sat on the edge, his crotch inches away from my heated face.

For a moment I forgot where I was or what I was even trying to accomplish. Wait, did he just say he wanted to work with Waterbridge-Howser? I realized my mouth had been hanging open, and I closed it with a snap. Adrenaline surged through my body. I had just closed a big account—this was massive.

"Sir?" I said, ignoring his position so as not to draw attention.

"Please, Kristen, it's Vincent. I let it slide when you called me Mr. Sorenson earlier, but if you're going to call me 'sir' then I'm going to address you as 'madam'. Now let's get back to business."

Vincent Sorenson, eager to get back to business. The irony wasn't lost on me, even in my dazed state.

"I can sign the paperwork today, but there's one condition." He paused. "You must be my point of contact. I'll need a number to reach you at any point in the day."

His dark pupils drew my gaze and I found myself unable to look away. I knew there'd be a catch. "Richard's usually the one who works directly with clients and I'm not sure I have the authority to—"

His expression implacable, he waved his hand to swat away my excuses. "Get the authority. Your partner is insulting and unacceptable. You're smart, ambitious, and not afraid to take risks. It's either you or I walk away."

I blushed at his compliments, although I wasn't sure why he thought I wasn't afraid of taking risks, but I had bigger issues to deal with. Even though this would be an enormous boost to my career, Richard would be offended if I agreed to Vincent's condition. Not to mention the obvious: I'd be spending much more time alone with Vincent. I doubted his true motives, but there was no way I could turn down this opportunity. I'd just have to figure out how to handle the complications.

I released a deep breath. "You're certainly very demanding, Vincent."

"You have no idea how demanding I can be." His eyes traveled up the exposed skin of my legs as if possessing me with his gaze. I crossed my legs to quell the uncomfortable sensation growing between them.

And there it is again, he can turn it on and off at will. Despite the edgy feeling of being this close to Vincent, I had to admire his ability to make anything sound sexual. If he was willing to sign with Waterbridge-Howser based on the misguided belief he'd get into my pants, I wasn't about to stop him. I'd just have to keep him at arm's length.

"Fine, I'll be your point of contact," I said, pulling out a business card from my satchel and handing it to him. "My information is on the card, you can reach me at the office during the day. My Blackberry number is available for *emergencies* as well." I hoped the emphasis was taken.

"Good," he said, pausing as though there was something else he wanted to add before gesturing towards my bag. "Do you have the paperwork?"

I handed him the contract.

"Thank you for deciding to go with us. I'm looking forward to working with you," I said, holding my hand out. He took it and squeezed firmly, the heat of his palm sending tingles up my arm. I didn't know if I was more excited about landing a huge client or Vincent's touch.

Without moving from his position in front of me, he signed and dropped the papers on his desk, rather than returning them to me. "Now that we have the business out of the way, we can get to the pleasure." The last word rolled off his tongue like a satin ribbon, sensuous and inviting.

"I'm sorry?" Heat coursed through my face.

"We didn't finish our conversation at the bar."

"I thought we were quite clear," I said, mouth drying by the second. He wasn't going to make this easy.

He shrugged. "You made it clear you didn't like mixing business with pleasure, so I didn't. The business is done, now it's time for pleasure."

As he leaned closer, his spicy cologne warped my brain into a puddle of incoherence. I froze as a series of lewd images played in my mind. His fingers caught a wisp of loose hair and pushed it behind my ear before trailing down my neck. Instead of pulling away, I closed my eyes and took a deep breath, hoping he couldn't read the desire painted on my face.

"If you read the paperwork, you'll see pleasure isn't part of the agreement," I tried.

Vincent took his hand away from my face, his dark pupils intense and focused. The sudden absence of his skin against mine felt wrong. I craved his touch immediately, but I tried not to lean closer to him.

"Of course not, the contract I signed was business. The pleasure part is just between you and me. Who's trying to mix them now?"

My pulse beat a steady staccato in my ears. Alarm bells ringing faintly in the back of my mind were overwhelmed by the building need radiating between my thighs. His sizable bulge was just a few feet away from me and became bigger every time I looked at it. I drowned in fantasies of being crushed under his chest, his cock pressing against my aching sex.

"Vincent, we can't."

"Why not?"

"I'll lose my job if anyone finds out."

He looked around. "How would they? I checked behind the couch earlier, we're definitely alone."

I had to give him credit for his persistence, but the longer I was in his office the more likely I was to give in. I needed to end this conversation quickly. I couldn't get involved with a man like Vincent.

"That's not the only problem," I blurted. "Just because you're attractive doesn't mean I'm willing to sleep with you."

Some of the intensity left Vincent's face and his mouth twisted into a boyish grin, but he never broke eye contact.

"You're attracted to me and I'm attracted to you. We're getting somewhere."

I flushed with embarrassment. It was an unintentional admission. "No we're not. There's no way I'm having sex with you in your office."

"I can pleasure you in so many ways beyond sex. Let me show you."

A surge of arousal made my body tremble. I had no doubt Vincent knew how to pleasure a woman. A man didn't become that confident without plenty of experience. In fact, he probably used the same lines on the perky blonde who greeted me earlier.

"What about your receptionist?" I snapped, the jealous words escaping my mouth before I had time to bite them back.

He furrowed his brows. "Lucy's a happily married woman and I've never touched her, nor would I ever. What kind of man do you think I am?" His tone surprised me; he sounded almost indignant.

I regrouped. "A dangerous one."

He shook his head and smiled. "I find danger only heightens the pleasure." His stance widened giving a fuller view of that distinctly male area so near my face. I gripped the arms of my chair.

God, he was determined. And worse, it was turning me on more than I'd thought possible. I licked my dry lips, realizing how close he was to me. Vincent tilted his face to the side, a lustful glint in his eyes.

He leaned down and pressed his thumb against my lower lip, dragging it open slightly. All thoughts of pulling away were drowned out by the roaring in my ears.

"This is wrong," I whispered, relishing his touch, my breathing shallow and forced. His beautiful face was close to mine, breath heavy and filled with desire.

"No, just a little dangerous."

His lips crashed into mine, sealing firmly over my mouth. My head swam, dizzy with desire. His tongue flicked against my lips, tenderly at first, then more passionately. I couldn't believe how full and soft his lips were. A soft whimper escaped my mouth.

This close to him, I could smell his unique scent underneath the cologne and feel his body heat. It was driving me wild. I squirmed in my seat, my panties beginning to feel damp already, and tilted my head back so as not to break the kiss. I knew if we stopped, my mind would return to rationality again, and that was the furthest thing from what I wanted.

He straightened, his lips drawing me upwards until I was standing as well. Faintly, I heard a stack of papers falling to the floor. We stumbled over to the leather couch in the corner. Our lips broke contact when I fell backwards onto the couch. My skirt rode up my thighs, revealing a scandalous stretch of skin.

"Gorgeous," he said, fire burning in his eyes.

I bit down on my lower lip as I tried to pull my skirt down to cover myself. Before I could adjust it, he was on top of me, his lips pressing firmly against my vulnerable neck, making me moan. I could feel his erection throbbing against my leg, his warmth seeping through the thin fabric. One hand slid up my inner thigh, and I instinctively spread my legs wider for him, urging him to touch me as my fingers fisted his wavy hair.

An electronic sound beeped from the desk. My eyes shot open and my hands fell from his head.

"Shit," Vincent cursed, running one hand through his hair and straightening his suit with the other.

He walked over to the desk and pressed a button on his phone. "Vincent, your three thirty is here. Should I send him in?"

"Give me another five minutes," he said into the speakerphone before looking back at me. "I'm sorry about the interruption. We can pick this up after work. I'll be done at five."

I stared at my surroundings, lightheaded. My skirt was just inches away from exposing my damp panties. I sat up quickly, smoothing it back over my legs. *What the hell did I just do?* I'd never lost my senses like that before and I was both mortified and furious with myself. This was completely inappropriate and unprofessional.

I got up to leave with what dignity I had left.

"Kristen, are you okay?"

I took a deep breath to control my temper. "This was a mistake Mr. Sorenson. It shouldn't have happened and I apologize for my part."

"Mistake?" His brows furrowed.

"I wasn't thinking clearly and you took advantage of it. We can still move on and pretend like it never happened, or I can transfer you to Richard—" My nails dug into the palms of my hands.

He let out a frustrated breath, shaking his head. "I'm not working with anyone else but you. I thought that was settled."

"Look, I admitted I'm attracted to you, but we shouldn't have acted on it. You're a client for Christ's sake. You caught me off guard and I was confused." I tried to make it sound as convincing as I could, but he didn't look like he was buying.

He stooped to pick up the paperwork and my work bag. As he walked over to me, I scrambled to my feet. My heels felt wobbly, and I took a step back, worried he was going to kiss me again.

He eyed me darkly, "Are you sleeping with anyone?"

He just wasn't going to give up. "No, but I don't—"

"Then there was no mistake. Stop apologizing, and stop denying what happened. We both wanted it." His brows narrowed, his gaze was intense. It was clear we were both exasperated, but for very different reasons. "If you still think you're confused, I'll make you a bet: before this week is done, you'll be touching yourself while thinking about me."

His casual reference to my masturbation routine left me shocked and wordless. Though I was no prude, I hadn't talked openly about touching myself to anyone but Riley and certainly not with any men I'd dated. And I wasn't even dating Vincent!

He watched my shocked expression as if waiting for me to speak, but I couldn't think of a coherent response.

"Right now I have a meeting. What I said earlier stands. If you're not my point of contact, I'm not doing business with Waterbridge-Howser." He gave me the signed contract and guided me to the door, his hand at the small of my back. I didn't have the energy to fight it. "This isn't over Kristen. We'll discuss later."

When I stepped out of the office, no one seemed to notice my shellshock or even pay me any attention. I let out a deep breath I hadn't realized I'd been holding and checked my reflection in the glass wall, one eye trained on the office staff. The collar of my blouse had been turned upwards and I quickly folded it down. I ran my hands over my skirt to smooth out the wrinkles, but my panties were a lost cause. I'd have to pick up a spare on the way back or do without for the rest of the day. As I ran my fingers through my hair, I could see my face was a shameful red in my reflection.

The sooner I got out of there the better. That kiss was a mistake that might cost me more than my career. Now that Vincent had seen the effect he had on me, I had a nagging feeling he wouldn't stop until he had exactly what he wanted.

Chapter Five

I studied my face in the Waterbridge-Howser bathroom mirror again, searching for traces of what happened in Vincent's office. It still didn't look right. For the third time, I wiped off my lipstick and reapplied. It had to look fresh, like I decided to redo it after getting the contract in anticipation of the big celebration. This was a huge deal. I should be happy.

During the walk back to the office, I'd decided I was going to remain his point of contact. Nervous as it made me, landing Vincent would be huge for my career. I couldn't let that opportunity slide. Even if I'd just let something almost unthinkable happen. A client had kissed me, and I had reciprocated. I knew he expected it to happen again, and I wasn't sure I'd be able to resist his potent sexual energy. It was irritating that a bad boy like him could have such an effect on me. Hadn't I told Riley I liked nice and caring guys?

I closed my eyes again. I was still embarrassed. This was a high point in my career, but I felt awful.

I gave my makeup and hair one final appraisal before deciding they were fine. I practiced my celebratory smile but it looked off. I'd never been good at being phony.

The door opened and two first-year analysts walked in. I couldn't wait any longer. It was showtime.

I walked out the door and Richard was waiting for me. "So how did it go?" he asked. His gray eyes were bolts of intensity. How on earth had he made it back from Jersey already?

I took a deep breath, put on my best fake smile, and held up the file. "The docs are signed. Deal's closed. We got it."

His hands shot up in triumph then came down awkwardly into a single clap. He looked torn whether or not to hug me but didn't, instead taking the documents from my hand. I let them go willingly.

He quickly leafed through each of the required signatures as I shifted back and forth on my feet. "See, I told you we impressed him. Carl will be pleased. God I can smell the bonus already. Definite promotion."

I nodded, smile still plastered on my face. The feelings stirring through my body weren't fit for expression. More than anything, I was beginning to feel anger. This should be my breakthrough moment; I'd worked so hard for it. Instead, I was concerned about hiding my relations with Vincent from my employer so I wouldn't get fired.

"You know, I was worried you were in there crying because something had gone wrong," he said, his eyes fixed on the final signature. "I'm surprised he didn't want me there for the signing. Did he say anything important?"

Before I could respond, a shrill voice came from our left. "Did I just hear we got Sorenson?"

I turned and saw the blonde curls and round face of Molly, another analyst. She had been at the company for five years and did good work, but hadn't quite broken through yet. Her voice also carried in a way I didn't think was possible before I'd met her. Not for the first time, I wondered if it could be heard on adjacent floors.

"Kristen and I locked it down today," Richard said, holding up the documents.

"Wow, congrats!" She turned and waved her finger at me. "Now you better make sure you don't let him take all the credit here. I saw you go to that meeting." Molly worked under a different manager and had known Richard long enough that she could get away with such comments.

I barely trusted myself to speak but I had no choice. Still with my best fake grin, I shook my head. "I won't."

"Well I won't stand for it if I hear you did."

I nodded, wanting to put an end to the conversation. While we'd been talking, heads had been popping out of cubicles offering their congratulations. The rest of the work day passed in a blur of emails and catching up on other work. It seemed everyone was excited but me. How could I have let Vincent kiss me?

I walked into my apartment emotionally drained; I wanted to collapse on my bed and cry. Riley was sitting in the living room watching one of the housewives shows and eating noodles. She waved when she saw me come in and finished chewing.

"How did it go?" she asked excitedly. I'd texted her on the way to the meeting with Vincent for moral support, but had forgotten about following up afterward. There would definitely be missed messages on my phone when I looked at it.

"We got it," I said wearily.

She screamed in delight, got up, and bounced over in her blue shorts and sorority t-shirt to hug me. I dropped my bag and reciprocated as best I could.

Riley seemed oblivious to my mood. "We *have* to go out and celebrate," she said.

"I don't know. I'm really tired."

"Come on! This is the biggest moment of your career. I would *kill* to have something like this happen at my job."

I looked at her and my shoulders slumped. "Sorry, I just need to wind down with a bath and fall asleep tonight. It was a really big day."

She looked at me and frowned. "Are you okay? Did something happen?"

Maybe someone. I couldn't bring myself to talk about it yet, so I shook my head. "I'm just totally beat. Stressful day."

I felt her gaze linger for a second longer but she moved on. "Okay. But we're celebrating this weekend and I'm *absolutely* not taking no for an answer. We can try that new tapas place. Sangria!"

I smiled. "Sounds like a deal."

Riley nodded and went to the fridge to get what was probably her seventh diet coke of the day. "So what actually happened in the meeting?"

I looked away. "It's kind of a blur. We talked, and after a while he was satisfied and signed. It's hard to remember the details."

"So this means a promotion, right? I remember you saying landing accounts was everything."

"Yeah, I guess."

I'd lied to my roommate. Remembering every second of that meeting was no problem at all. The problem was forgetting.

I went to my bedroom to change into my robe before walking into the bathroom. As I drew hot water for my bath, my thoughts lingered on Vincent. The audacity he had to kiss me in his office had me stuck between upset and impressed. I supposed it was to be expected from an adrenaline junkie like him. Obviously most of the risks he'd taken up to that point had worked out just fine. If this one failed, it was no sweat off his back. I recalled the incident in Cape Town. Compared to being bitten by a poisonous spider, kissing a girl was nothing.

I shrugged off my robe and poured my favorite bubble bath soap under the tap. The cinnamon candle I chose was one of my favorites, and I lit it while waiting for the tub to fill up. Once it had, I turned off the tap and stepped in, submerging myself up to my neck.

The warm water and fragrant scents had an immediate effect on my nerves. I'd chosen bubbles with notes of vanilla, sugar, almonds, and just a hint of musk. The combination was relaxing while making me feel sexy— something I needed because I wasn't getting anywhere with my dating life. Or lack thereof. It'd been a long time since I'd even kissed someone, let alone had to resist a kiss. I'd forgotten these things take willpower.

I leaned back and closed my eyes, feeling the bubbles pool around my chest and neck. This was just what I needed. I wiggled my toes and started a body scan meditation I learned in yoga class, gradually relieving the stress from my system.

As I felt my muscles relaxing, I shifted and realized how sensitive my pussy was. *When did that happen?* I hadn't been this aroused in weeks. Images of Vincent's profile invaded my mind. His arms. His chest. And his waves of blonde hair inches above my face earlier that day while I was sprawled beneath him on his couch, his probing fingers raising my skirt to my hips. He felt even better than he looked.

I was vaguely aware of my hand sneaking toward my aching sex. When the pad of my finger touched my clit, I paused. Masturbating about Vincent wasn't going to make this any better. I needed to forget my attraction to him and think of him only as a client. Maybe I should ask Riley to set me up with a date or two; she'd love the opportunity.

As if seeing other men would solve my Vincent problem. I smiled when I remembered him calling Richard "Dick" at the end of our first meeting. Bad boy or not, he was gorgeous, charming, and had a sense of humor. Forgetting my attraction to him would be like forgetting to breathe.

Maybe one touch. I let my hand graze my clit lightly, stimulating the sensitive nerves there. My breath caught and I tilted my head back. It'd been a few days since I last touched myself, which was normal. But since I met Vincent, days felt more like months. I tried another touch and an unexpected shiver ran up my spine, making me gasp. I'd anticipated a slow build, but after a few light strokes, I realized I was already primed.

He'd bet me I'd masturbate to thoughts of him. The gall of Vincent Sorenson. I always thought I'd be offended if someone said anything so crude to me, but it only heightened my attraction to him, which was annoying. I wanted to resist and prove him wrong—more for my own conscience than his—but I was rapidly becoming too aroused to care. What would it matter anyway? I'd never tell him and he'd never know. He wouldn't have the satisfaction.

Without wasting time, I continued pleasuring myself, increasing both the pressure and area with each stroke until I was gliding up and down my lips in a slow circuit, coming up to my clit and down, easing in and out of my aching sex. Fingers steadily at work, my thoughts went back to Vincent. The fantasy of his strong hands exploring my body with his signature boldness drove me wild. My breath started coming in quicker bursts as I shortened my motion, an orgasm swelling in my core.

My phone rang, interrupting the moment. On the second ring, I realized it was my work phone. At eight-thirty. Nobody called that phone after work unless it was important, and I was expected to answer no matter where I was.

Drying my hands on my towel, I leaned out the tub and reached into my robe—reflecting, not for the first time, on how ridiculous it was I had to take my work phone into the bathroom with me.

Strange. Whoever was calling had an unknown number.

"Kristen Daley," I answered.

"I hope I'm not catching you at an awkward moment." The familiar voice made my pulse leap.

Vincent. I became all too aware of my compromised state with him on the other line. Why did this have to happen to me?

I was tempted to hang up, finish my orgasm then call him afterward with a clear head but I wouldn't know what number to dial. I took a deep breath hoping to calm my nerves enough that my voice would come out evenly. "Mr. Sorenson, of course not. How can I help you?"

"You know it's Vincent," he said, correcting me. "I'm afraid I have a problem."

My heart skipped a beat. There were numerous problems he could have, one of them being regret for signing with my employer earlier today. "What problem are you having?"

He sighed deeply into the receiver. "I haven't been able to focus on my meetings or get any work done. You're constantly on my mind. I need to taste your lips again. Uninterrupted."

I tried to think of something to say, but first had to find the pieces of my mind that had scattered across the bathroom.

"I'm flattered. But that sounds like a personal problem that I can't help you with, Mr. Sorenson."

"Vincent. And tell me if you haven't thought about me as well."

I briefly wondered if my company recorded conversations on this phone but remembered IT telling me they didn't. Regardless, I needed to steer this discussion away from lips and tasting. "*Vincent*, I'm sorry, but this discussion just isn't professional." I didn't understand why it was so hard for him to get that into his head.

"Then let's end it. We're two consenting adults who have a strong sexual attraction for one another. What do we have to do to make this happen?"

A curious bubble swam towards my chest and I popped it with judiciousness. "As an adult, I admit our mutual attraction, but you and I can't happen. Personal relations with clients are forbidden by my employer. If you have a problem with that, speak to the Waterbridge-Howser human resource department."

"I already checked. There aren't any rules against it."

Damn it, he was determined. "There are office politics. I could get fired or dead-end my career—I hope you understand that. You might not have anything to lose, but I do."

"I'm losing my mind thinking about you." The urgency in his voice was surprisingly endearing. It was both unsettling and relieving to know I had such an acute effect on him. "I felt the way you kissed me. You want more."

My hand at my forehead, I closed my eyes and sunk lower into the tub as I tried to control my rapid breaths. "Vincent, it was a heated moment and we both got carried away. That's all."

His voice became dark. "Have you touched yourself yet?"

I hesitated, my grip on the phone tightening. "That's really none of your business." My response came shakier than I'd wanted and I silently cursed myself.

"Already," he purred, the silky vibration raising goosebumps across my skin. "Kristen, let's be reasonable about this. I promise you the real thing is better than whatever you're imagining."

I squeezed my thighs together to suppress the growing need between them and sighed. "Please don't make this so hard."

"I am hard," he grunted then paused as if thinking, and when he spoke next his gruff voice was dripping with desire. "You're naked right now, aren't you?"

My toes curled against the drain cover. *How did he know that?* His ability to sense my arousal through the phone was uncanny, and I briefly wondered if he could also read my mind. "Nice try," I lied, a smile creeping across my face despite myself. "But I need to get going, if that's all."

"God, Kristen. If you're touching yourself right now it's only a fraction of the pleasure I'd give you." He sounded as pained as the throbbing ache growing between my legs. "You're selling both of us short."

His strong words had an even stronger effect on my body. I was afraid I was going to start touching myself again if I didn't get off the phone. The need was becoming overwhelming with him on the other end of the receiver; he was so far away yet so close.

I exhaled deeply, preparing the words I needed to say to him. "As your advisor, I recommend you hang up the phone, then with that same hand pleasure yourself until your arm goes numb or you're satisfied—whichever comes first. Once you've finished, you'll have forgotten all about me."

When he didn't respond, I began to wonder if my brush-off was too harsh. Then he spoke. "I made the right decision to have you as my point-of-contact. You're everything I expected and more. We'll be in touch."

I heard a click then silence. I looked at my phone a second before putting it back in my robe pocket. What did he mean I was everything he expected and more? Was that whole conversation just some kind of weird test? The idea annoyed me further.

I sighed in frustration. The sexy-relaxing combo I'd been working with wasn't going to cut it anymore—all relaxation had gone down the drain with that call. I needed a glass of wine and my bed. It had been a long, long time since I'd been this horny. My entire body felt like a wound spring.

I swung my leg over the side of the tub, intending to get out but gasped at the sensitivity. My sex, forgotten during the heat of the conversation, was swollen with desire. Knowing I wouldn't fall asleep without release, I rocked back into the tub and kicked my legs up. My fingers returned to where they'd been before and I resumed stroking, eager to flush myself of an irritating ache that had only grown worse during Vincent's call.

I thought of Vincent on top of me, the way his strapped arms would look as they braced his weight, the feeling of his rough grip, the raw power of his lithe body stretched out.

My strokes became shorter as my orgasm neared its peak. *You're naked right now, aren't you?* His lurid accusation intensified the stimulation and I increased my pace until the sensation was unbearable. The next second I felt the first shudders of the most powerful orgasm I'd ever had rip through my core. I gripped the edge of the tub to brace myself as I trembled with relief and satisfaction.

After a few small aftershocks, I came down from my bliss. My head was clearer than it had been moments ago and I assessed the situation. There were worse things than having a hot billionaire obsessed with you. If I could keep my actions in check, working with Vincent would be great for my career. On the downside, he was seductive as sin and persistent to a fault. I briefly imagined all the women willing to do anything he asked of them. A bad boy like him could really hurt me, and if anyone should've learned that lesson, it was me.

I got out of the tub and dried off. It was already getting late and I was more than ready to slip beneath my covers to end this exhausting day, but my mind wouldn't stop racing. After tossing and turning in bed for an hour, preoccupied with thoughts of Vincent, I grumbled in resignation.

I reached into my nightstand, grabbed my vibrator, and went for round two.

Chapter Six

The next few days went by in a haze. After the thrill of landing the account, it was back to the normal grind of the analyst life: making reports and parsing data to pass along to higher-ups. I stayed busy in an attempt to stop myself from daydreaming about Vincent. My next meeting with him wasn't for a week, and I didn't want to think about him any more than I had to. Doing so was too distracting and more than a little stressful.

Still, at the end of each day, I was disappointed not to have heard his voice. It seemed like Vincent was going to pursue me harder but maybe he had already found a new distraction. Of course, that would be a stress relief from a professional perspective—and should have been one I welcomed wholeheartedly—but I had to admit his pursuit of me was the most exciting thing that had happened to me in a while. Maybe ever.

Finally, Friday rolled around. When I got home, Riley told me she scored some tickets at work for the Knicks game and asked me to join.

I quickly pulled on a nice shirt and skinny jeans but took longer on the makeup and hair. I was applying the final touches in the bathroom next to Riley who was finishing her makeup.

"So have you seen Vincent since Monday?" she said, touching up her mascara in the mirror.

"Nope," I said. "Our next meeting isn't until next Tuesday."

"Is he still into you?"

"What do you mean?"

"Come on. The question isn't whether he's into you, it's how aggressive he's being about it. You get all flustered every time I mention him, so spill. I know you're hiding something."

"I'm not. You saw him. He's hot. Lots of girls find him hot, and I'm sure he does really well with plenty of them. But we have a professional relationship."

She blinked her eyes a few times and put her mascara away. "Okay, if you don't want to talk about it, that's fine. But he's into you and I know you know."

"Whatever. Who are we meeting again?"

She'd moved onto lip gloss and smacked her lips a few times. "Jen and Steph. They started at the same time I did. I think you've met Jen."

Riley had a lot of friends from work and I'd probably met this girl before even if I didn't remember. I was just happy to be off the subject of Vincent. "I think so. Are we meeting them there?"

"Yeah, and they texted that they left a minute ago. You ready?"

"You know I'm always faster than you. Let's go."

"After you doll."

The seats weren't great, but they were cheap, and more importantly it was a low stress, girls' night out, which was exactly what I needed. We got popcorn and sodas and settled in, flirting lightheartedly with the guys in the row in front of us. Jen and Steph were both fun and inclusive, filling me in when the conversation referenced inside jokes stemming from work.

The three of them had a better rapport than anyone I worked with at Waterbridge-Howser. The work sounded less interesting from what Riley had told me, but at least the environment sounded fun.

Ten minutes into the first quarter, we spotted ourselves on the Jumbotron. The camera lingered long enough for us to wave and cheer enthusiastically. It was funny how excited I was about something so trivial; for the tenth time that night I reflected on how good Riley was being to me. This kind of evening was absolutely perfect. She often knew when I was upset and steered things to my comfort zone when I needed it—and I needed it as much as ever after such a crazy couple weeks. Even though she didn't know all the details, she had a good idea of how I was feeling and wouldn't push the subject further than my comfort level.

During the break between the first and second quarter, we were approached by a balding man in a suit with a nametag that indicated he was a member of the hospitality staff at Madison Square Garden. "DAVE" touched his hand to his earpiece, then looked between me and Riley.

"Excuse me, miss," he said to me, "are you Riley Hewitt?"

Startled, I pointed to my friend. "No, that's her," I said. Riley turned to face Dave.

"Ms. Hewitt, you and your group have been upgraded to box seats, compliments of the house. If you'll follow me."

We all looked at each other in shock. Did we win some kind of random drawing? When Dave indicated he didn't know the details, only that he was the messenger, we briefly discussed it among ourselves. "Why not?" was the verdict. I'd never been in the box seats at MSG—they were super expensive—but it sounded like a blast. After the craziness of the situation with Vincent, my luck was looking up; this night was somehow getting better by the minute.

After a short walk, Dave led us through a private hallway to a double-doored suite. Passing through the threshold, we stepped onto lush carpeting and marveled at the leather couches surrounding a wall-sized TV displaying the game. In the back laid out buffet-style was enough snack food and drinks to stock a grocery store. Our mouths beginning to water, Dave continued the tour by ushering us through a sliding glass entrance to a balcony. He gestured to the rows of seats indicating we could watch the action live if we preferred but we were mainly interested in returning to the food.

He brought us back inside and clapped his hands together. "That concludes the tour. Any questions?"

"Are you sure this is all free?" Riley asked. "Like you're not going to charge my credit card after we leave right?"

Dave smiled. "Somebody's getting charged but it isn't you fine ladies, I assure you." After we indicated we had no further questions, he turned to leave but said, "I almost forgot. You'll be joined later by some Knicks shareholders. I promise, they're wonderful company." He winked then left with a sordid grin on his face.

Oh great. The mystery behind a group of girls receiving too-good-to-be-true box seats became clearer.

Jen huffed. "If this 'upgrade' means getting hit on by a bunch of old guys all night, I'm going to be pissed."

"I don't know," Steph said. "If they're shareholders, they're probably really rich. Let's just take advantage of the free goodies, have fun, then go home."

Jen went to the suite door and checked to make sure it wasn't locked, which thankfully it wasn't. After some discussion and some longing glances at the food, we decided to stay and enjoy ourselves.

We stuffed our plates with nachos, cookies, and other hip-friendly treats and brought them out to the balcony seats. By the time we settled in, the second quarter had already started. The Knicks were losing, but that didn't bother me. I was more of a football girl but crowd energy made watching any live sport enjoyable. Plus, the delicious nachos kept my tummy happy.

A Knicks player threw yet another terrible pass and the other team stole it for a breakaway dunk. The Knicks coach called timeout and slammed his clipboard down, venting his frustration in the form of passionate words and wild gesticulations.

"Reminds me of my boss," Riley remarked.

"Totally," said Jen. Steph nodded in agreement.

"I thought you said he wasn't bad," I offered.

Riley rolled her eyes. "Compared to others, he's not. But he has a habit of always walking by, making sure no one's playing solitaire or checking Facebook. He's a stickler for rules and blows his top when people don't follow them. If I had to describe him with one word, I'd say 'particular'."

Her boss sounded similar to Richard on a bad day. "I'd use a stronger word. 'Anal' sounds good."

A warm hand rested on my shoulder, making my words linger in the air. "Hello Kristen."

I twisted my head to see who it was even though the voice was unmistakable. Vincent, in a crisp white shirt that bolded his dark eyes and slate-gray slacks that hid powerful lean muscles, was preparing to take a seat in the row behind us. The impeccable timing combined with being hit by his intense aura made my nacho-filled stomach drop to the floor.

"Vincent, what are you doing here?" I asked anxiously, unsure which parts he caught of our private girls conversation. *Besides stalking me.*

"You remembered to call me Vincent. I'm touched." He smiled then squeezed my shoulder gently. "I was enjoying the game from the front row when I saw you and your friends on screen. I figured I'd send my regards to my new account manager."

"You're his account manager, Kristen?" Jen asked, surprised.

I looked at her, then Steph, then Riley. Their eyes trained on Vincent were as wide as their mouths, like they'd just seen a god. "Umm . . . yeah. Guys, this is Vincent Sorenson, CEO of SandWorks. He's a new client." I introduced Jen and Steph to him and he shook their hands in turn. They looked as if they were going to melt from his touch and I couldn't help commiserating.

"Although we hadn't been formally introduced, Kristen's already told me about you Riley," he said smoothly, shaking her hand.

She blushed then giggled uncharacteristically. "Kristen's told me all about you as well."

I glared daggers at her, hoping she'd take the cue.

"Good things I hope."

"Only the best," she replied, pointedly ignoring me. "Jen, Steph want to get some more snacks inside?"

I stealthily pinched her hip and she smoothly pulled my hand away without reacting. She was determined to leave me and Vincent alone and I was determined to prevent that. God knows what happened last time Vincent and I were by ourselves in his office. I shuddered to think something similar would happen at this public venue.

"I'll come with you," I said, more as a plea than a suggestion.

"Oh no, I'm sure you guys have *so* much to talk about." She smiled at me then turned to Vincent. "Thank you for the box seats Mr. Sorenson. Hopefully Kristen can show you our *full* appreciation." Her obvious wink made me wince. Then she tugged Jen and Steph inside, the two of them stealing glances at Vincent as they left.

When it was clear we were alone, Vincent deftly hopped over the row and took the seat beside me. He reached back and grabbed two drinks he must've put there before alerting me to his presence and offered one to me.

"A mojito. I know it's your favorite."

Irritated by the charge I got from being so near him, I accepted the drink and took a gulp to calm my nerves. I wanted to be mad at him but couldn't think of a good reason. "See what you did? You scared off my friends." This was supposed to be girls' night out, but with the amount of testosterone he exuded I sensed it had just turned into Vincent's night out.

"They seemed to be having fun." He raised his glass and clinked it against mine. "So do you." His lips curled into a charming smirk and he adjusted his position, brushing his arm against mine. The unwelcome surge over that entire side of my body made me realize how much I missed his physical presence.

I took a sip, then another, debating what to say to him while he eyed me suspiciously, the drama of the game below us all but forgotten. "Do I make you nervous?" he asked.

His relaxed posture and collected demeanor provided a stark contrast to my own composure. "No. Why?"

"You're pounding that drink."

I glanced down at my mojito which was now just ice cubes. *When did that happen?*

His amused eyes were on mine when I looked back up. "I can get you another if you want."

"Are you trying to get me drunk?" I blurted, recalling our last heated conversation in which I was naked and in the middle of masturbating. "I'm not going home with you tonight if that's what you're planning."

"Relax Kristen. You're a beautiful, intelligent woman. I know you can handle yourself." The casual way in which he deflected while complimenting me made me stiffen and when he put his hand on mine, I felt my knees go weak. Good thing we were sitting down. "What's really bothering you?"

I placed the drink in the cup holder and pulled my arms across my chest, more to avoid the effect of his touch than to pout. "You. What are you doing here? Are you stalking me?"

"I may constantly fantasize about you but I don't follow you around or have you followed if that's what you're asking."

"So you just happened to be here when I'm here."

"It's the playoffs. As a major shareholder in the team, I have more reason to be at this game than you. Maybe you're the one stalking me?"

His cleverness caused me to laugh and I gained a greater appreciation for his sense of humor. "You wish."

"Maybe you researched my finances, realized my connection to the Knicks, and, unable to resist your intense feelings, showed up hoping to see me. Looks like we both got lucky." He took a sip of his own drink while keeping his dark eyes trained on me.

Even though I'd been plagued with constant thoughts about him throughout the week—some of them including fantasy meetings in his office—I couldn't imagine myself acting on them. "In your dreams, buddy," I said, my tone more playful than serious.

He leaned toward me, his mouth close to my ear and his long velvety hair brushing my cheek. Rather than resisting, I found myself relishing the contact. His scent was different than usual but the signature spice was present and had its usual effect on me all the same.

"You want to know what I dream about? We can make that a reality," he purred.

My body involuntarily shivered at the silky vibration. I admired his graceful tenacity but I had already come to expect that from him. "Sorry, but you're not really my type."

He pulled back but was still close enough for me to feel his radiating heat. I saw his seductive smile widen. "I am. But what do you think your type is?"

"Nice. Sweet. Caring. Not exactly a thrill-seeking CEO."

His smile turned lopsided and he replied, "You'd be bored in a month. I think you want someone exciting who also makes you feel safe. I can do that."

My thumb and forefinger pinched my chin in thought. "Hmm . . . you know that does sound appealing but as enticing as it is, I already told you, we can't happen."

"Professional concerns, I know."

I raised a brow. "So you do listen."

"When it involves your lips, you have my full attention."

The tension in my shoulders relaxed and I felt a crack in my guard. He was both physically beautiful and demonstrating thoughtfulness. It wasn't just the drink and remembering my roommate; he actually listened to my concerns. I decided to illustrate the situation to ensure we were on the same page. "You're Romeo and I'm Juliet. If we get together, bad things will happen."

"Is that it?" He carefully scanned the arena then returned his powerful gaze to me. "Because I don't see your bosses anywhere. I thought a Waterbridge-Howser employee would be a little more creative when it comes to getting what she wants. You certainly strike me as the type."

"What type?"

"A woman who gets what she wants. Harvard for economics? Working at a wealth management firm trying to get ahead when guys like your partner, Richard, are trying to screw you over or just screw you at every opportunity? You have to be both tough and smart to thrive in that environment."

How did he know what I studied in school, or even where I went?

As if reading my mind, he said, "I looked up your background before I signed with your company. Remember, I'm trusting you with hundreds of millions of dollars."

"I thought you made me your point-of-contact just to get into my pants."

"I might be a risk-taker when it suits me, but I'm not a moron. You're an impressive woman, Kristen."

Well at least he knew how to make a girl feel good. And aroused. He shifted his legs closer to mine and in that moment, I could swear the alcohol must've reached my brain because all I could think about was the image of him ripping off those slacks in front of me like a male stripper. "Do you try to have sex with all the other impressive women you meet? Is this a conquest for you?"

He looked at me with surprise. "None as impressive as you."

"Well, I'm flattered." I really was, but my purposeful tone didn't show it.

"I don't see you as a conquest," he added. "But I'd be lying if I said I didn't find your feistiness a turn-on."

I blushed fiercely. "I have legitimate concerns."

"Which brings us back to the topic you didn't address. If all you have are professional concerns, it won't be an issue keeping what we do just between us. We've kissed in my office and you still have your job."

He had a point, but there were other reasons I was resisting him, and I wasn't about to surface those skeletons. "It's a risk I can't take. As deliciously attractive as you are, I want my job more than I want you. I barely even know you. And you barely know me."

"Then get to know me. Give this," he gestured back and forth between me and himself, "a chance."

"What are you saying?"

"A date. If it goes well, let's have more. If not, we go back to a purely professional relationship. I promise, keeping one date a secret won't be a problem." He found a lock of my hair and curled it seductively between his fingers. "What we do is private. My lips are sealed."

As exciting as the prospect of a date with Vincent was, his suggestion seemed inconsistent with his approach. Until now, he only seemed interested in having sex with me. Dating was a whole different beast and I wasn't certain he grasped the significance. "Vincent, as thrilling as a date sounds, I'm not sure you understand what you're proposing. A date isn't sex. And if we went on one—not saying we would—but if we did, I'm telling you upfront we won't be having sex. Maybe not even kissing." The last part was added for emphasis.

I expected him to pull back but without skipping a beat he said, "I'm fine with that."

His response gave me pause. "Did I miss something? I thought you just wanted a quick lay."

"I spend the average week on three different continents so I don't usually have time for a relationship. Hence, the direct approach. You've made it clear you aren't the kind of girl who wants casual relations. I still want to see you. Taking it slow isn't what I'm used to but I can adjust."

"Is your concept of dating just a means to sex? I'm no prude but to me sex is a meaningful act between two people who share a connection. I'm not just going to add an extra hurdle for you to clear. You just raved about how smart I am and now you're treating me like I'm an idiot."

"Dating is whatever we make it. I want to show you I'm interested in you beyond just sex."

His response was a relief. "Okay."

"Is that a yes?"

Probably the result of the mojito coursing through my veins and Vincent's pheromones swimming in my brain, I heard the words come out my mouth before I had time to process the implications. "Fine. One date."

His stunning features lit up making him even more gorgeous.

"But," I added, cutting off the words lingering on his tongue. "I need discretion. I don't want to worry about my employer finding out about us."

"I agree, it won't be an issue. How's eight tomorrow?"

"In the evening?"

"No, a.m."

"Isn't that a bit early for a date? What do you have in mind?"

"It's a surprise."

My head was spinning. "Okay . . . where do you want me to meet you?"

"I'll pick you up."

I nodded. "How can I know what to wear if you won't tell me where we're going or what we're doing?"

"Nothing fancy, don't worry about it," he said, looking me up and down. "It looks like you know how to handle that anyway."

My face grew hot again. "Thank you."

He leaned close to me, and I felt his breath on my neck and shuddered, bracing for an attempted kiss. "Just be ready at eight. You can do that, right?"

"Yes."

"You don't think I'm going to try to kiss you here, do you? You're underestimating me, Kristen." He leaned back into his chair, grazing my leg with his fingers as he did. His touch sent a jolt through my body, making my breath hitch.

"I can behave," he finished.

I looked at him, breathing in short bursts. I hadn't thought it was possible to look intensely calm before that moment.

"I'll get you another drink."

As he went into the suite he passed Riley on her way out. She bounced down next to me. "So that looks like it went well."

I snorted. "I guess."

"So when's your date?"

I had to work on being less obvious. "Tomorrow."

"Good. If you said there wasn't a date I was going to smack you."

I turned to her. "You do know I'm still allowed to make my own decisions, right?"

Riley cocked her head. "Sometimes you need a little push to make the right one. Where's he taking you?"

"It's a surprise. He wants me to be ready in the morning."

Riley crinkled her nose. "Doesn't sound like the usual, whatever it is. Something tells me he's not the kind of guy to invite a girl to walk around the park."

"No, definitely not."

"It's one date. Worst case scenario, you probably get to do something exotic and fun with a guy who is stunning eye candy."

I swallowed. "Worst case I lose my job."

She laughed. "If bad boys got caught easily, they wouldn't still be bad boys. You'll be fine."

The rest of the game passed in an increasingly tipsy blur. I spent the evening waiting for Vincent to touch me again from where he sat behind me—my shoulder, my neck, anything—but he never did.

As we left the arena, the only thing on my mind was the next morning. What could he possibly have planned that required starting so early?

Chapter Seven

My alarm clock buzzed at 7:00 a.m. I woke up face down on my pillow and promptly chided myself for taking full advantage of the complimentary bar in the suite last night. I drew my comforter over my head, desperate for the extra sleep, when I realized I was going on a date in an hour. A surge of anxiety pulsed through me and I shot from bed, shedding my clothes on my way to the shower. I turned the water on hot, hoping the heavy steam might relax me, but I couldn't stop wondering what a surprise date with Vincent Sorenson involved. Rented out museums? Five-star restaurants? Yachts? I had no idea what I was going to wear.

I lathered up a bar of soap, running it across my torso and down my legs—shit, should I shave? I was planning on wearing jeans but I could hear Riley's voice in my head, berating me for my informal outfit choice; she would insist on a skirt and I would eventually yield. I grabbed my razor and swiped the blade carefully over my legs.

I turned off the shower and grabbed a towel, quickly drying off before rummaging through my closet to find a modest blue skirt and a silken racerback tank top. I threw them on over a matching bra and panties set and walked into the kitchen to find Riley sipping liberally from a cup of coffee and flipping through *People*.

"I'm sorry, did I wake you up?" I bypassed the coffee, already jittery enough from nerves, and poured myself a generous cup of orange juice.

"Are you kidding me? I've been up for an hour, there was no way I was going to miss this."

"Well you wouldn't have missed much, I still don't know where we're going."

She closed her magazine slowly and pushed it away before looking at me in contemplation. "Are you bringing condoms?"

"What?" I asked, the abruptness of the question catching me off guard.

"This," she said, "is why I got up early. You have to think about these things!"

"No, Riley, I am not bringing condoms. It's only our first date. A test date really."

"Well, I commend you. It would take some serious restraint to keep me from tearing the clothes off of a guy like Vincent."

I rolled my eyes over the rim of my cup. "Are you sure you don't want to go on this date for me?"

"Come on, I was kidding. I'm just excited for you," she said. "It's your first official date in—"

"Don't remind me," I interjected, cringing at the thought that it'd been two years since my last relationship and months since I went on anything close to a date.

"You're ready for it, that's all I'm saying."

"Yeah, I think I am," I said softly, remembering my tryst with Vincent in his office, the way I had practically collapsed into him as he kissed me. I couldn't remember a time when things had felt so natural.

"Well, the outfit is definitely cute," Riley said, giving me a quick once-over.

"I thought you'd approve."

"But I hope you plan on using a comb before you leave." She laughed and gestured to the knotted curls my hair had dried into.

I glanced at the clock and darted to the bathroom when I realized I only had a few minutes left to get ready before Vincent was supposed to arrive. I grabbed a brush from the sink and tamed my hair into a stylishly messy bun, finishing just as a knock came at the door. I jumped in nervous anticipation and quickly applied a coat of mascara to my eyelashes.

"He's here!" Riley sang out from the living room, her voice a high trill. She ran into the bathroom and ushered me out, thrusting my purse in my hands. "Have a good time, be safe, and tell me *everything*."

"I will, I will," I reassured her as I opened the front door. She escaped back into her room before Vincent could spot her in her pajamas.

He stood in front of me, six feet of muscled perfection fitted in jeans and a sleek black sports coat. He gave me one of his lopsided smiles and my heart skipped a beat. "Good morning," I managed, suppressing the bashfulness that had suddenly overwhelmed me.

"You look great," he said, placing his hand on the small of my back and guiding me out of the apartment building. I could feel his fingers gripping at the fabric of my shirt, the familiar gesture sending a flush of heat to my face.

When we got outside we stopped in front of a silver Camry, its square frame and dull paint job suggesting its old age. I'd expected a limousine or fancy sports car, something befitting his wealth. "Is this your car?" I blurted.

"You wanted discretion," he said as we got in.

"Is this the part where you tell me where we're going?" I teased as he began driving.

He shot me a grin. "Do you always make it this difficult for a guy to surprise you?"

"I like to be prepared, that's all."

"It shows. Those charts you put together for our first meeting must have taken some time."

I looked at him, dismayed, as I recalled my disastrous performance in Cape Town. "Turned out to be worth it, I think they were the only redeeming part of our presentation."

"Are you sure that little slip and fall act wasn't planned?"

"I told you it was a mistake, but Richard will probably be implementing it into our future meetings."

"I can't blame him, it was my favorite part."

"So you told me, but I'm not sure I want to be known for groping CEOs." I tried not to sigh as I remembered the firm expanse of Vincent's chest beneath his t-shirt.

"I guess I was just lucky I was there to break your fall." He turned to me smiling, and I practically had to tear my gaze from the curl of his full lips.

"Something tells me you don't trip over your own feet often," I said, distracting myself from the lustful gleam in his eye. "Don't surfers need to have pretty good coordination?"

"In that case, we'll have to work on yours," he said as the car came to a slow stop.

"What?" I looked out of the window, taking in the hazy tarmac of an airport parking lot.

"We can't go to St. Thomas without surfing at least once."

I clenched my jaw to keep it from dropping to my chest. I had to fight the urge to protest, running through all the reasons surfing made me nervous in the first place. But I knew I couldn't sabotage a date with Vincent Sorenson because I was too afraid to stand on a board for awhile. "Is this JFK?" I sputtered as we got out of the car.

"It's a private airport, actually. There weren't any direct flights to the Caribbean so we're settling for something more intimate." He gestured to a small plane in the distance.

I had imagined the yachts and the sports cars, but I hadn't been anticipating a private jet. Maybe Vincent wasn't the bad boy I'd pinned him for. In fact, he was turning out to be pretty considerate. A date on a remote island couldn't have been easy to organize and his little stunt at the Knicks game was more than generous—my friends certainly thought so.

"Well, I do like a challenge," I conceded, deciding if he was willing to make an effort then so was I.

He grabbed me by the hand and pulled me towards the plane. "That's what I thought."

I had just been getting used to the idea of a private jet when I was met with custom leather seats, a glass coffee table, and a suede sofa all situated in the cabin of the plane. True, I hadn't been on a date in a long time, but even if I had been, it wouldn't have been anything like this. Dinner and a movie this was not.

"So much for discretion," I said as I surveyed my surroundings.

"We'll be all alone up here," he said as he turned to me, his eyes falling briefly to the line of cleavage visible at the neck of my shirt before traveling back to my face. I glanced around, looking for a stewardess, but he wasn't lying. The cabin of the plane was empty except for us—it couldn't have been more discreet.

"Is it customary for CEOs to have their own private jets?" I was trying to sound nonchalant but I knew my awe was glaringly obvious.

"I admit, it takes some getting used to." As we settled into our seats he placed his hand on the armrest between us, his long fingers splayed across the leather. I wanted to reach for it, to bring the knobs of his knuckles to my mouth and run my tongue over the shallow lines in his skin. I glimpsed the couch, imagining the small of my back sticking to its leather surface as Vincent leaned over me, the pressure of his muscled frame pushing me deep into the cushions. He would draw my legs around his waist, his hand cupping the space behind my knee as our lips opened around one another. I would grab his lean hips and push myself against him, eager for a friction I hadn't felt in a long time.

"You mean jetting overseas isn't one of your pastimes?" I swallowed, trying to pull myself from my heated reverie.

"SandWorks wasn't exactly handed to me. I spent a lot of time traveling, working paycheck to paycheck, before I thought of the waterproof camera. In fact, that Camry is something of a relic from those days."

"I have to admit, it wasn't what I was expecting when you picked me up."

"I did a lot of traveling in that car, even spent some nights in it," he said. "But when business took off one of the first things I had to learn was how to manage my money."

"Isn't that what you hired us for?" I couldn't imagine him struggling to learn anything. His business savvy had been obvious since the first day we met.

"Yes, but it wasn't always easy to know who to trust in the beginning so I had to rely on myself. Something tells me you never had much of a problem with that, though."

"What do you mean?" I asked, growing defensive at the implication.

"Financial analyst, Harvard girl—your parents must have done well for themselves to be able to send you there."

My home life wasn't a point of conversation I enjoyed but I didn't want him thinking I hadn't worked hard for my success. "My parents put a lot of pressure on me to do well, but they couldn't afford private school. I left Texas with some savings from summer jobs but I had to work my way through college; I didn't pay off my student loans until I landed a job at Waterbridge-Howser."

"Texas? I knew I could detect an accent."

"So could everyone in Boston, I spent a lot of time trying to hide it but I guess I got tired of pretending it wasn't a part of me."

He turned to me, his gaze smoldering. "You're a walking contradiction."

"Excuse me?"

"You say you don't like to take risks, but it couldn't have been easy starting a new life on your own."

I had never considered myself adventurous, my own parents thought it was irresponsible of me to uproot my life, but Vincent seemed unconvinced.

"You're not exactly easy to figure out either. Vagabond turned CEO? I didn't see that coming."

He gave me one of his sly grins. "You can't be prepared for everything, Kristen."

A few hours later we landed, the white beaches and swaying palm trees greeting us from the airplane window. We made our way through the small airport to the rental car area. Vincent picked out an Aston Martin convertible, which surprised me probably more than it should have considering I'd just stepped off his private jet. I dealt with wealthy clients on a daily basis and I had some vague idea of the luxuries they could afford, but I'd never actually been wealthy myself—seeing what Vincent's money could buy had thrown me off a bit.

The drive to the beach served well to distract me from my nagging fears about surfing—the breeze whipping my hair, the taste of the ocean's salt lingering in the air, and the rolling hills that surrounded us were impossible not to notice. But as we approached a wood slatted surf shop edging the beach, the creeping fear I'd felt earlier came back full force.

"I have to admit, I'm kind of nervous about this," I confessed as we got out of the car. "Jellyfish, sharks . . . you hear horror stories, you know?"

He took my hand, gripping it reassuringly. "Don't worry, I'm not going to let anything happen to you."

Vincent was right, he had been surfing for years, and I really didn't have any reason not to trust him—with my safety at least.

"But you can't surf in that," he said, gesturing to my skirt and blouse. "We'll need to get you a swimsuit."

After trying on a few swimsuits in the dressing room, I decided on a black halter top bikini with single string bottoms.

My heart nearly sank to my stomach when I caught a glance of the total price of our surfing gear—between new swimsuits and surfboards, Vincent had spent more than Riley and I spent on restaurants in a month.

After I had changed, I met Vincent by the water and was nearly floored by the man who stood waiting for me fitted in nothing but a pair of white boardshorts that clung loosely to his hips. My eyes lingered on his six-pack, the taut ridges of his abdomen leading down to the sharp, downward angle of his pelvic bones. I swallowed as I noticed the nipple rings glinting from his chest and among the various tasteful tattoos around his right arm and chest there was a blackened outline of a diamond on his rib cage. I wondered about its significance; Vincent might have been a risk taker but there always seemed to be a purpose behind everything he did.

I stumbled in the sand, wrestling with the side of me that was salivating over his edgy look and the side of me that was a little intimidated. I'd never been with a man who took so many risks with his body, but I'd also never been with a man who defied all of my expectations. Not to mention a man who was so irresistibly attractive.

His lips slowly curved into a smile as he eyed me up and down. "I like the swimsuit. Ready?"

I had to force my gaze to meet his. "Ready as I'll ever be."

We waded into the ocean, the shallow waves leaving rivulets of water trickling down Vincent's bare chest. When we were waist deep he dropped our surfboards by his side and turned to me.

"The most important thing to understand is you have to control your board, you don't want to find yourself overwhelmed by the force of the wave," he began. "So lay down on your stomach and put your hands here."

I did as I was told, sliding my stomach across the board's waxy surface.

"Now press your hips into it." Without warning he gripped the soft curve of my hips and pushed against them, the callouses of his fingers working against my skin. The way he effortlessly maneuvered my body until it was in the correct position made me think I wasn't the first woman he'd taught how to surf.

I tried to bite my tongue but I was determined not to be just another one of Vincent Sorenson's conquests. "How many surfing lessons have you given?"

"A few."

"Mostly female clientele?" I shot, the words coming out before I even had a chance to consider them.

He pulled his hands from my hips, the heat of his skin lingering where his fingers had been, and I instantly regretted my presumptuousness.

"Are you trying to ask me how many girls I've brought here?"

I sat up on the board, straddling it to keep from falling over. His eyes wandered to the water lapping over my clenched thighs. "I just want to know what this is."

"This is a date, Kristen. Not a ploy. The only lessons I've ever given were just that—lessons."

I averted my gaze. "It's not your conventional first date, that's all."

As my board began to drift, he pulled it closer, his fingers brushing the flesh of my inner thigh. I shivered at the contact and considered maybe it wasn't anger I was feeling but jealousy. If Vincent's touch could send me into a fit of desire then I could only imagine what he'd made other women feel, ones who didn't demand first dates.

"What are you used to?" he asked.

"What most people are used to—dinner, movie. I guess I haven't gone out with enough CEOs."

"Who have you gone out with?"

I shifted away from his touch, growing uneasy at the one question I refused to breach. "No one serious," I said as I leaned forward on the board so I was laying on my stomach again. "Am I doing this right?" I asked, determined to change the subject.

"Move further down the board and keep pressing your hips into it."

I wiggled down the board and awkwardly extended my abdomen but I was too flustered by the thought of my messy dating history to focus on my form. Suddenly Vincent was behind me, his hands settled into the groove of my hips as he pulled my body toward him. I wished desperately I was wearing a t-shirt, a wetsuit, anything to lessen the direct contact between us. I couldn't distinguish between the water and the dampness that had been growing between my legs since I first caught sight of him on the beach.

"I can't—" I began to protest, too overwhelmed by a foreign desire to think about surfing technique.

"You can. I'm right here." He slid his hand to the small of my back and pressed. My pelvis pushed into the board, the vague contact with my clit sending a heat into my belly. I chided myself for my desperate arousal—I wanted to take things slow, especially with Vincent, a man who was too busy continent hopping to commit.

I pushed myself up again, distraught. "I have no idea why you like this sport so much," I said, trying to blame my agitation on the lesson. I teetered on the board as I tried to gain my balance and he clutched the top of my thighs to keep me steady.

"Haven't you ever had an adrenaline rush?" he asked, moving his hands further up my thighs until they were dangerously close to the heated space between my legs. I looked at him, his eyes wild with anticipation, the tendons of his neck taut as he clenched his jaw. "Your body becomes attuned to every sensation, your energy peaks—"

"It's addicting," I breathed.

"Don't you want to feel that way?" he asked as he drew his face closer to mine, our lips brushing briefly. I could taste the salt that had caked to his mouth.

"And if I fall?"

"It won't hurt."

I pulled away from him, afraid if I let him any closer I'd lose my bikini, and paddled toward the shallow waves in the distance.

We practiced surfing well into the afternoon but Vincent proved more of a distraction than a help—the pent up sexual energy I had felt during our lesson still lingered within me. When my arms were too weak to keep paddling, we left the water for the beach. As I set my surfboard in the sand, Vincent reached out and gently grabbed my left hand, pulling it close as if to inspect it.

"How did you injure your pinky?" he asked, sitting down next to me. Being so close to him on the sand made me pine for the cooling effects of the water. "You've been holding it out all afternoon."

I pulled my hand away, instinctively clutching my finger. "I'm a little accident prone, tripped and fell a few years ago and sprained it."

"Accident prone? You were pretty good on the water."

I practically scoffed, I'd been falling off my surfboard all afternoon. "I don't think surfing is my true calling. It's a little too rough for me out there."

"Sometimes rough is good," he said as he lifted my hand to his mouth and kissed my pinky, dragging it across the full line of his bottom lip. I looked up at him, the sun catching the amber of his eyes, and I could hear the rapid beating of my heart in my ears. I still didn't understand how one look from him could throw me so off balance. I glanced around the beach, making sure we were alone.

"You're covered in sand," he said, wiping the grainy pebbles from my palm. "We should rinse off."

I did feel the need for a shower after all our time in the water so I agreed.

He stood and reached his hand out to me, pulling me up and into him. My hands grasped at his bare chest as I tried to gain my balance. His skin was warm and slick with a layer of sweat, and I couldn't help but imagine running my tongue down the firm ridges of his abdomen. It had been two years since I'd slept with a man and I could feel my neglected need hitting me full force.

I tried to pull myself from his grasp, afraid the friction of our bodies would overwhelm the rational part of me, but he grabbed me by the waist and pulled me closer. The quick pulsing of my heart seemed to take up between my legs as he leaned forward and took my face in his hands. As he pressed his lips into mine, working my mouth open with his tongue, my knees buckled and I grabbed his bicep to keep myself steady. I could hear his heavy breathing, feel his warm exhales against my cheek as our tongues moved over one another. It was true it had been years since I'd been with a man but I'd never been so consumed by a kiss and I was worried I wouldn't be able to control myself if I let it continue.

"Where are the showers?" I asked, breaking away. I was desperate for a reason to distance myself from him—what would he think of me, better yet what would I think of myself, if I had sex with him when I'd demanded a date to avoid sex? But without a word he lifted me onto his waist, my legs wrapping instinctually around him, and walked us toward the showers.

"Put me—" I began but he cut me off with another kiss, his mouth pressed so urgently against mine that my lips tingled. I ran my fingers through his hair, pulling lightly, as the hard cut of his pelvis rocked against my clit while he walked. I clenched my thighs around his torso to keep myself from grinding shamelessly against him, wanting to feed the desire that had begun pulsing faintly between my legs.

He put me down as he turned on the shower and before I had time to get my bearings, I felt his hands running down my back and across the waist of my bikini bottom. He reached up and loosened my hair from its ponytail, the heavy, damp locks falling down my back as he rinsed the sand from my body.

"What are you doing?" I asked, trying to avoid his touch. I immediately berated myself for getting caught up in the moment—I didn't need casual sex, especially with someone who was used to getting what he wanted from women. I had promised myself I wouldn't get involved with another man too quickly, and here I was about to strip naked on the first date.

"I'm cleaning you."

"I can do it myself," I insisted.

His hands stopped their merciless roaming but lingered in the middle of my back, his fingers batting at the loose strings of my bikini top. He looked at me, the water running over the sharp bridge of his nose and down to his lips. "Why're you so afraid to ask for help?"

"Because I don't need your help." I tried not to acknowledge the muscled torso, wet and glistening, just mere inches from me.

"I want to make things easier for you." He slid his fingers beneath the strings of my bikini top and I could feel him wiping away the coarse sand stuck there, his fingers moving toward the side of my breast. I felt my nipples harden from his touch, barely concealed beneath the thin fabric of my suit.

"I just think it would be better if we take things slow," I breathed.

"Is this slow enough?" His hands creeped toward my chest, the cool tips of his fingers sending goosebumps across my skin. Just as he was about to cup my breast, he shifted quickly, trailing his fingers lightly down my torso. I groaned in a frustrated desire, wanting him to pinch my nipples between his fingers, take them between his teeth and bite gently.

I reached out to him in spite of myself. My fingers traced the raised edges of a tattoo on his shoulder. "What does this one mean?"

"It's sanskrit for 'balance.' I'm a hard worker, Kristen, but I believe in rewarding myself." I could feel the bulge of his stirring package beneath his board shorts as he moved closer to me.

"And these?" I crooned as I fingered his nipple rings.

"Something of a souvenir from Fiji."

"You couldn't just get a t-shirt?" I leaned into his chest and took his nipple between my fingers, pinching the cool metal ring lightly.

"I wanted something a little more interactive," he moaned as he grabbed a handful of my hair.

"I knew I felt something hard when I fell on you in South Africa." The aching throb between my legs had become nearly unbearable and all I wanted to do was pull his board shorts from his hips and take him in my hands. But things were already going faster than they were supposed to and I would have no one to blame but myself if I gave into Vincent and ended up getting hurt.

"What about you, Kristen? Any piercings you're hiding from me?" The tone of his voice and the ceaseless roaming of his hands suggested he had every intention of finding out unless I put a stop to things.

I tore away from him, mustering all of my willpower to deny my desire. It was hard to ignore just how sexy Vincent was, and I wasn't sure I believed those surfing lessons he was giving were innocent. It seemed like a flawless plan—the minimal clothing, maximal touching and his persistent charm, any woman would succumb to the seduction. But I wasn't looking for seduction and if that's all Vincent was interested in doing then it was better I walked away from our date with my dignity still intact, something my last relationship had taken from me.

Not wanting to cause an argument or dredge up my relationship history I flashed him a doe-eyed look and stepped out of the shower's stream. "Nothing worth pursuing comes without patience," I teased.

His shoulders dropped in obvious disappointment but the toothy smile on his face left me hopeful that maybe sex wasn't his only motive. "I guess that means you want to see me again."

"Maybe," I said playfully as I left the stall, "but you'll have to let me off this island first."

I made my way to the women's bathroom and slowly peeled the soaking swimsuit from my body, taking my time as I tried to decompress from the shower. It was ridiculous to try and convince myself I didn't want Vincent. But whisking a woman off to an isolated island for an afternoon had raised some red flags. Although no one had ever planned such an elaborate date for me, I was starting to think Vincent knew the rules of seduction far better than he knew the rules of dating. I didn't want to give up on him but I couldn't let my body get the best of me next time.

Once I had changed and fixed my hair into a loose, damp braid I left the bathroom to find Vincent leaning against the convertible, the deep tan of his skin standing out against his white t-shirt.

He leaned down and kissed me before tugging lightly on the braid. "You look beautiful," he said.

I blushed, conscious my makeup had washed off and my hair was a mess. "You don't look so bad yourself."

"Are you hungry?" he asked. "All that time in the water wore me out." He shot me a suggestive grin and I knew he wasn't just talking about the ocean.

"I'm starved," I said, but I knew no amount of food could quell my appetite.

Chapter Eight

By the time we boarded Vincent's plane, it was evening and I was physically drained. After the hours of surfing, we tried out a Caribbean barbeque place with amazing burgers then drove around the island sightseeing until the sun set. It was a romantic, memorable first date and I found myself hoping it wouldn't be our last. I'd expected him to be his usual charming and seductive self all day, but he was surprisingly attentive and caring, showing he'd listened when I'd told him about taking things slow. He suggested we stay the night—in separate rooms of course—but I wanted to avoid the possible implications. Resisting him in the public shower was hard enough; sleeping in the same hotel with beds conveniently nearby might've been too much for my resistance if he decided to be seductive again. Instead, I'd fallen asleep on his shoulder on the flight back. When he dropped me off at my apartment, we exchanged a chaste goodbye kiss. He promised to text me tomorrow and I promised to tell him what I thought about a second date. I trotted to my room and plopped on my bed, exhausted from the day's activities.

***

Monday morning felt better than it had since as long as I could remember. With everything I did with Vincent over the weekend, it seemed like forever since I got the chance to sleep in. Which is why I took full advantage of the opportunity on Sunday. Except for exchanging a few flirty texts, the day had been uneventful but relaxing. Not that being involved with Vincent Sorenson wasn't thrilling enough, but the lazy Sunday was just what I needed to re-energize.

I'd told him I needed more time to think about seeing him again but it was more to save face than anything else. If I was honest with myself, the idea of secretly dating a gorgeous client was thrilling, but I'd been careful not to reveal that to Vincent. I also found myself wanting to know more about him. He wasn't the surfer bum that Richard pegged him for nor was he the cold, calculating businessman typical of individuals his stature. He was something in between. Steadfast in pursuit but adaptable. Charming yet respectful. In other words, complex.

Next weekend seemed interminably far away. What would we do on a second date? Where did we stand? All I knew was I already felt safe with him, which was both comforting and unnerving. I hadn't felt that way in a long time with anyone; I'd even begun wondering if I could trust a guy again.

I recapped my date to Riley expecting irrational excitement, but her reaction was subdued. She announced she was coming down with a cold, her throat's scratchiness since coming back from Cape Town an advanced indicator. Before leaving for work, I told her I'd stop by a Duane Reade to pick up orange juice and cough medicine. If she needed anything else like blankets or a humidifier, she could just text me.

I arrived at work a little earlier than usual, eager to start the day. The morning passed in a blur of investment research and excel sheets. It was rare that coworkers didn't stop by to chat but I supposed it was just one of those busy mornings. I was about to head to lunch when Richard made an unexpected appearance at my cubicle.

"Hard at work, I see." His voice didn't contain its usual confidence bordering on smugness.

"Just finished the ROI projection charts for the Sorenson account and about to head to lunch. Need something?"

He sighed heavily and I leaned back in my chair preparing myself for some bad news. There was no way the firm had found out about my trip with Vincent already. "I came to tell you that you've been promoted."

"What?" This was good news. I had been promoted only six months ago, which earned me the privilege of working under Richard in the first place. Now I was promoted again? Richard had been right, landing the Sorenson account did have its perks.

I beamed. "This is great! It's just like you said. So are you going to buy that new convertible you've been talking about?"

"No." He sighed again, rubbing his temples with his fingers. His jaw was working overtime. "*You* have been promoted. Not me. I also found out Vincent specifically listed you as his point of contact. Did you know about that?"

I gulped. Richard was upset with me and I had to diffuse the situation. Complete honesty wasn't the answer. "He mentioned the possibility, saying he was impressed by my work. But I didn't know he would go that far."

His eyes narrowed. "What did you tell him and what did he say when he handed you the signed documents?"

"I just went through the standard follow-up pitch and he stopped me before I could finish. He said he liked my work and wanted to sign the papers. I gave them to him and didn't really look too hard after he signed."

He opened his mouth to say something but shut it, his mind seemingly deep in thought. He grumbled something under his breath and left before I could question the situation or offer words of consolement.

I tried to put Richard's frustration into perspective. Despite him being ten years my senior, my promotion brought me to the same level as him. No longer a meager 'analyst', I was now a 'client acquisition manager' that would be reporting to Richard's boss, Carl Stansworth, directly. I figured Vincent's request for me to be his point-of-contact was the reason Carl promoted me, but I wondered why Richard wasn't promoted. Richard certainly did his fair share of work, which meant either the company wasn't doing well enough to promote him or Richard wasn't on Carl's good side. I figured it was the latter. Whatever the reason, the situation made it look like I stole his client lead. I was concerned about rubbing Richard the wrong way, but there wasn't much I could do about the circumstances.

I skipped to lunch and returned to my desk with a newfound passion for my job. My fingers a whirlwind at the keyboard, I felt at peak productivity, churning page after page of reports and analyses.

It was approaching the end of the workday when my purse chimed with the sound of a text message. I reached inside, flutters in my stomach, figuring it was another flirty text from Vincent. I was already thinking about him so often since our date it was difficult to concentrate on anything else, and the frequent communication wasn't helping. I wasn't sure how long I'd be able to resist him if we kept this up.

I discovered the text was actually from Riley. Maybe she needed something else from the store.

Hey someone stopped by asking for you.

Not what I expected, but okay. Using my thumbs, I typed a response back to her. *Did he have dark eyes, sexy blonde hair, and abs to die for?*

A moment later the chime sounded. *No. Didn't get his name.*

So it wasn't Vincent. He probably wouldn't have dropped by anyway knowing I would be at work. I also wasn't expecting any packages . . . who could it have been? I was in the middle of preparing a response when I received another text. Riley must have accidentally hit send early on the last one.

But he had gorgeous blue eyes, brown hair, and rimless glasses.

Suddenly, the office spun, coming choppily like a film with missing frames. My pulse leaped and I felt an immediate tightness in my chest. I tried to breathe but couldn't. The familiarity of the experience made me realize I was having a panic attack. I stared at the words, reading and rereading them, hoping they'd change.

Blue eyes. Brown hair. Rimless glasses.

There was no mistaking it. *He* had shown up at my doorstep. How did he find out where I lived? Why did he show up now? Should I call the police? Run? Stay at a hotel tonight? For how long? A flurry of questions and actions raced through my mind. And none of them seemed good.

In the midst of the chaos, my phone chimed again. Hands trembling, I checked the new message, fearing the worst.

The sight of Vincent's text grounded me in reality. *I'm aching for you. When can I see you again?*

I recalled how safe I felt around him. That was the one thing I desperately needed right now and only he could give it to me. Not knowing what else to do, I decided to see him tonight, be with him.

Tonight. Your place. Can you pick me up after work?

I waited anxiously for his response. A few seconds later, it came.

What happened to slow? :)

I'm not promising anything. Can't a girl come over just for fun?

Of course. We'll hang out.

Spotting Vincent's car pull to the side of curb, I checked to make sure nobody I recognized was around. Once I confirmed that none of my coworkers would suspect Vincent was taking me to his place, I hopped into the passenger seat.

His peacock blue shirt showcased his trim torso and his tailored black pants matched his expensive shoes. The effect was striking, and for a moment it felt surreal that a guy like this was picking me up from work.

"Hey." I smiled at him.

He shifted the car to 'park' and leaned over, kissing me as if starved for the taste of my lips. His raw hunger for me was intoxicating. Hesitant at first, I easily succumbed to the sensation, running my hands through his long blonde locks and reciprocating. I enjoyed the soft feel of his mouth and his surprisingly fresh masculine scent.

Once our lips broke contact, he spoke. "Hello, Kristen."

Hello to you too. "Sorry to give you such short notice."

He placed his hand on my bare knee, the warmth from his skin a welcome sensation. "Anytime you need anything, don't be afraid to tell me. I can be accommodating."

"Thank you." I considered for a moment if I should tell him about my ex-boyfriend showing up at my apartment, but I didn't want to freak him out. People typically didn't unload their baggage onto someone else when they've only been on one date. I hadn't told anyone about my ex's dark side before, not even Riley. But then again, I hadn't had to. "So how was your day?"

"Went from good to great." He grinned as his hand began lightly brushing my leg below my skirt. "How about yours?"

"Not bad."

His sharp eyes studied my features carefully. "You seem kind of tense. Is everything all right?"

I hesitated. "I got a promotion today, thanks to you."

"Congratulations. You deserved it," he said. "And I'm not just saying that because I like you. You're a rare talent."

I blushed. "And you're quite the seducer. You sure know how to flatter a girl."

"Not flattery. Honesty. And I'll take that first part as a sign of affection."

The sound of my stomach grumbling betrayed my hunger and Vincent must've heard it. "What do you feel like eating tonight?" he asked. "I'm planning on cooking for us."

"No preference," I answered. "You don't have to go through all that trouble though, I was just thinking we'd go to a restaurant or get take out."

He shook his head. "I'm taking you to the best restaurant in the city—my kitchen. Tonight's an opportunity to impress you with my culinary skills."

"Expert surfing instructor, now a master chef." Also, billionaire and sex god, but I figured those were already obvious. "How many surprises do you have?"

Those sinful lips forming a smile made me feel a sudden ache between my legs. "Oh the things I'll show you, Kristen."

Just as my thoughts began to turn naughty, a mental shopping list interrupted them. "I almost forgot, I need to pick up some medicine for Riley. Do you think we could get that first?"

"Of course. We'll stop by the grocery store," he said, pulling away from the curb to join the flock of cars in traffic.

If picking me up from work was surreal, grocery shopping was an illusion. I was cautious at first that someone might see us, but caution turned to laughter as we roamed the aisles for items. Two weeks ago I was rebuffing Vincent's advances, and now we were picking out food to cook for dinner like an established couple. It was a domestic experience that felt bizarre but natural. I hadn't been looking for anything serious or Mr. Right or even much of anything, and there I was with someone who felt like all those things. I hadn't expected Vincent to be this way but then again he'd been constantly surprising me.

By the time we left, I felt a lot better than when he had picked me up from work. With half a dozen bags loaded into his trunk, he drove while I played the role of navigator, directing him to my apartment.

When we neared my place, all humor and playfulness evaporated from my system, replaced by the anxiety from earlier. He turned to me and smiled as he stopped the car in front of my apartment building, putting the emergency lights on. "I can park. I'm curious to see your place."

"It won't take long, I'll just be a minute," I said, hopping out. I didn't want to risk him running into my ex, if he was still around. Things would go from bad to disastrous. "Keep the car running."

He seemed a little confused but then nodded. "I'll be waiting."

As I scaled the wooden steps of my building's stairwell, I couldn't help checking over my shoulder every few steps or being wary of dark corners. I breathed a sigh of relief when I reached my door without incidence. When I entered the apartment I found Riley in a robe on the sofa watching television, a box of tissues next to her.

"Brought you some stuff," I said, handing her the orange juice and Dayquil.

"Thanks, you're the best." Her voice was nasally and she blew into a tissue to clear her nose.

"Do you have the flu? Should I take you the doctor?" I put the back of my hand up to her forehead to check her temperature.

"Nah, I think it's only a cold. I just need to keep blowing my nose every few minutes."

"Glad to hear it's not serious."

She looked at my shoes which I hadn't taken off like I normally would when I entered the apartment. "You going somewhere?"

I suddenly felt guilty for bailing on her. "Riley, I'm going to stay at Vincent's tonight."

Her eyes grew wide. "Oh, congratulations! I'm glad to see you're finally coming out of your dating shell."

"About that . . . I need to tell you something." I waited until she gave me her undivided attention. "Don't open the door for anyone. Especially if it's the guy who came by earlier. Whatever you do, don't let him inside."

Her brows furrowed. "Who is he? Should I be worried?"

"He was someone I dated before I moved here. Don't worry, he only cares about me; he won't do anything to you. I'll tell you more about it some other time. But keep your mace handy just in case."

"Whoa, whoa." Her hands made shoving motions in front of her face. "You can't just say 'keep your mace handy' and dash out. What's going on? Do we need to call the cops?"

I shook my head. "We can't call the police. It's complicated." As reluctant as I was divulging details that had haunted me for the past two years, I briefly told her about Marty and how he hurt me. How he was the reason I moved from Boston to NYC in the first place. I didn't have the time or desire to elaborate on sordid details, but she deserved some sort of explanation.

She looked at me with concern as if I was the sick one. When I didn't explain further, she sighed and said, "Okay, Kristen. You can tell me the rest later. I'll keep an eye out."

"Thanks for understanding, Riley."

"When are you coming back?"

"Maybe tomorrow. I'll bring you some more goodies."

She sniffled. "All right, stay safe."

"I will."

I went to my room and quickly changed out of my work clothes into a comfy pair of jeans and a light blouse. I packed an extra set of clothes and my toothbrush into a night bag.

When I finished packing, I waved to Riley and left the apartment, returning to Vincent's Camry.

"Is your roommate all right?" He sounded as concerned about Riley as I was. "I can drive her to the hospital."

"I appreciate the thought, but she just needs sleep and vitamin C."

"You're not sick are you?"

"I don't think so."

Before I could react his lips were on mine again, this time parting my lips with his tongue. He probed my mouth with slow licks of his tongue against my own. Caught up in the heated embrace, I momentarily forgot my concerns.

"Good," he said after our mini makeout session ended. "I'd hate to miss work because I couldn't stop myself from kissing you."

The engine started and we headed toward his place. It was only a few blocks away but with the rush hour traffic in Manhattan it would take us twenty minutes.

We stopped at a red light. I glanced out the window and saw someone on the sidewalk with brown hair and rimless glasses. The hairs on my neck stiffened. It looked like him, but wasn't. Fidgeting in my seat, my hand began rubbing my pinky again.

"Something wrong? You look nervous." Vincent's voice startled me.

I shook my head. "I guess I'm just looking forward to seeing your place."

He grinned. "That makes the two of us."

We pulled into his underground garage complex that resembled ones built for malls. It was filled with exotic cars. With my minimal knowledge on the topic, I was only able to identify a half dozen Lamborghinis and Corvettes but I was still impressed by the eye-catching designs of the ones I couldn't name. After a few loops to the lower levels, we found an empty spot and parked.

Still in awe, I asked, "How many people live in your building? There are a lot of expensive cars here."

He smiled. "Just a few tenants. Most of these are mine."

"Oh." Realizing he could've picked me up in any of these much nicer, much more expensive cars, I had a greater appreciation for his being discreet about our involvement. The Camry was far less luxurious than the Lamborghini.

We stepped into an elevator and Vincent inserted a key into the control panel. The trip to his floor was both faster and quieter than I anticipated. I'd expected a hallway leading to his front door, but when the elevator opened I saw a grand piano and a pair of sand-colored plush sofas around a glass coffee table on dark hardwood flooring illuminated by elegant accent lighting—we were already in his living room. We were on the south side of the building, but the spacious layout enabled sight across the apartment to the north side windows where I could see the Chrysler building as well as the rest of Manhattan. One step out the elevator and I realized the entire building floor was his apartment.

"Impressive," I said, slack-jawed.

"Glad you like it," he said smoothly, leading us deeper into the living room.

I set my bag on the floor and took a seat on his couch as he carried the grocery bags into the kitchen. He returned with a glass of white wine wearing slippers instead of his black loafers.

"Should I take off my shoes?" I asked, not seeing the pile of shoes I was accustomed to seeing when entering my apartment. Instead, there were a bunch of modern abstract statues on display, making this place seem more like a showroom than a personal living area.

He eyed my flats. "You can just put them next to the couch, make yourself comfortable."

In the middle of taking my shoes off my stomach growled again, which was his cue to begin washing vegetables in the kitchen.

"What are we eating?" I hollered. We'd picked up a lot of things, some serious and some just for fun, like a box of Teddy Grahams. It was probably more than we needed and I wasn't sure what he planned to cook for dinner and what he planned to save in the freezer.

"It's a surprise."

"Do you need any help?" Not that I was a great cook myself, but I could at least cut vegetables.

"There's not too much prep work. It'll just be a few minutes. Feel free to look around and make yourself at home. "

Looking around was exactly what I wanted to do. "Are you sure you don't want to give me a tour? I might see something embarrassing." I cringed at the thought of Vincent seeing my bedroom. He'd find papers littering my desk and undergarments hanging on chairs and strewn across the floor. It wasn't that I was messy; I just had my own organization system.

"Like what?"

"Oh I don't know. Underwear, stuffed animals, porn, sex toys."

He was silent for a moment. "Just don't look too hard then."

I couldn't tell whether that was a joke or not but decided I didn't want to ask. As I went from room to room, I noticed everything was neatly arranged and clean, far from your typical bachelor pad. I wondered if he had a maid keep his apartment tidy or if he did it himself. Knowing him, it was another line on his already impressive résumé—accomplished housekeeper. I took a moment to muse the fantasy of him being a manservant.

When I found his office, I spotted documents on his desk that were thoroughly highlighted and marked with detailed notes. Curious, I sifted through them and recognized they were the ones I gave him during our first meeting. I put a lot of work into those documents. He must have thoroughly studied them before deciding to choose my company as his wealth management firm and making me his point-of-contact.

At the beginning of my self-guided tour, I couldn't help making comparisons between Vincent's living style and Marty's. They were both neat and meticulous. But towards the end I found some movie posters of martial arts films from the 80s. That cheesiness was decidedly not like my ex.

By the time I circled back to the living room, fascination with Vincent preoccupied my mind. Besides the posters and getting to see his wardrobe of suits, I was disappointed not to find many more personal items. It seemed as if he had moved in recently. He did mention traveling multiple times per week, so maybe he kept the family pictures somewhere else.

He had an elaborate kitchen though, fit for a top chef. I was pulled toward the food by the wonderful smell.

"Have a seat in the dining room. I'll bring the dishes out," he said untying his apron and hanging it on a nearby rack. He was still in his work clothes, but traded black loafers for sandals.

When I took a seat at the table, there were already two glasses of white wine set out with the tableware.

"Something fresh and light." He entered with two plates in hand.

I smelled the mouthwatering scent before I saw it. Linguine al dente with shrimp scampi. The presentation was immaculate. "My favorite seafood dish. How did you know?"

"It's my favorite as well. I guess our tastes match."

"Maybe with food. But I think we differ on the decor." I gestured to the Bruce Lee poster sitting in the corner.

"It's an old keepsake." He smiled and handed me my plate of shrimp and noodles. "Try this. Tell me if I got it right."

I took a bite then had to take another one. "Wow this is delicious. Where did you learn to cook so well?"

"When I was right out of college I surfed a lot with a few of my buddies. We had seasonal jobs and worked just enough to support our lifestyle. To save money, we'd buy food for the group and I ended up being the one to cook most of the time; the others weren't very good at it." He laughed.

"I can see why they wanted you to cook." I scarfed down another bite. "That wasn't too long ago if I'm not mistaken. So what's it like to go from that kind of lifestyle to this in only a few years?" I gestured to the lavish apartment.

"It's been a rollercoaster ride. Perfect for a thrill-seeker like myself. Now, instead of being responsible for cooking for a group of guys, I'm responsible for thousands of employees. The stakes are different but fundamentally it's the same."

"Do you still keep in touch with those guys?"

"We try to get the group together at least once a year. Everyone's busy these days, not just myself. A few of them even have kids." He laughed and shook his head as if remembering something ridiculous. "If you knew them back then, you would think they were destined for life-long bachelorhood."

The obvious inquiry was on my mind. I didn't want to ruin an already wonderful evening, but I knew it would bother me if I didn't ask. "And how about you?"

He paused for a moment which made me almost regret asking the question. "Being a bachelor has its benefits. I travel a lot and do a lot of thrill-seeking activities. Being unattached makes it easy to do those things. But I'm thinking it might be more enjoyable to do things with someone you care about."

"Makes sense."

"How about you? The life of a single-female wealth manager, meeting rich, handsome clients seems appealing."

"I haven't really given much thought to settling down. I hadn't really even given much thought to dating in the past few years. Been mainly focused on my career."

"Are you saying I'm special?"

"Don't get a big head, Mr. Iron Chef," I teased. "You're persistent. I'll give you that."

"That's not the only thing that's big right now," he said, his hand settling on my thigh and rubbing slow, suggestive circles with his thumb.

Unsure if I was ready for things to progress further, I tried to change the topic. "What are we having for dessert?" I asked, more as a joke than a serious question. The exquisite dinner he prepared was more than satisfying, and his domestic skills scored major points in my book.

He didn't answer, but smiled and went to the kitchen. I waited a beat, not sure whether I was supposed to follow or remain seated. When he came back he had in his hand a red cloth napkin. "I want you to taste it. But you're going to need to put this on first."

"A napkin? Messy desserts don't sound like your style."

His smiled widened. "Try again, beautiful."

I examined the napkin again, noting that it was folded twice over into a narrow band suitable for wrapping and tying. "Umm . . . a magic trick?"

"Blindfold."

"I think I must've missed a part of our conversation."

"You're going to put on this blindfold and I'm going to feed you the dessert."

"Why do you want me to put on a blindfold?" I'd never done this before and I was a little anxious.

His grin was both mischievous and seductive. "It'll help you isolate the sensations in your mouth."

"Can't I try it without the blindfold first?"

"If you want to taste my dessert, you're going to have to follow my rules. Trust me. Just like you did in Cape Town."

"You haven't been planning this have you?"

"From the moment you pinched my nipple, a lot of things have gone through my mind. This could have been one of them." I could hear the amusement in his voice and wondered what other ideas he entertained that day. "I noticed you've been tense since you left work. I want you to forget about the stress."

He moved my chair—with me in it—from the dining table and placed it in the open area nearby. He came up from behind me and brought the blindfold in front of my face, preparing to place it over my eyes. My pulse quickened at the thought of having my eyesight taken from me. The last time I trusted him, I ended up holding a poisonous bug. "You're not going to put a spider in my mouth are you? Because if so, I can't continue with this," I asked, half-serious.

"Don't be silly. If anything, you'll be begging me to continue." The dark warning sent a shiver of arousal through me.

He put the blindfold on and tied it firmly behind my head. It was tight enough not to shift around but loose enough to be comfortable. I tried reaching out to touch him to ensure he was still there; he took my hands and gently placed them on my thighs. "Hands in your lap, until I say otherwise."

In complete darkness, I felt uncomfortably vulnerable. I'd never done anything like this with anyone before. Was I ready to trust him this much? I sensed him leave the room for a moment to go to the kitchen. All I could do was wait for what he would do next.

Then his footsteps returned and stopped in front of me. "Open your mouth."

Here it comes, I thought. I tentatively obeyed, unsure what was coming. What was he going to feed me? The sound of a metal clink made me think of a belt buckle. Surely not . . .

"Wider."

I wasn't sure if I should have; I probably should've asked him what he was going to put in my mouth. Instead, my lips stretched wider, compelled by the authority in his voice.

"Be careful with your teeth. I don't want you biting me."

What? Before I could protest, something slowly entered my mouth and sat heavily on my tongue. It tasted sinfully sweet and creamy.

"Close."

Without needing be told, my lips instinctively wrapped around it and tightened, suckling the decadent chocolate from his finger.

"Taste good?"

My murmur of approval sounded more like a moan. As he slowly retracted his finger, I took my time licking the tip, wanting to savor every last bit. I heard him stifling a groan when he finally pulled away. It was one of the most erotic sounds I'd ever heard, and I desperately wanted to remove the blindfold to see his expression.

"That was just the first bite." His voice registered lustful amusement, his mouth close to my ear. "This time, I want you to really focus on the pleasure in your mouth. Block out everything else." I felt him brush my hair intimately behind my ear then his tender lips were against my cheek. "Like this," he whispered, his mouth trailing gentle, sensuous kisses to my ear, drawing soft moans from my lips. "And this." He pinched my earlobe between his lips and pulled the sensitive flesh into his mouth, sucking it with just enough pressure to make my legs quiver and sex clench in heated anticipation. There was no way I'd be able to block out the sensation of those lips on my body. And I didn't want to.

"Ready?" he asked.

I wasn't but I wanted another taste of the dessert to heighten the pleasure from his kisses. "Yes," I breathed.

Eager, I opened my mouth again. Sweet cream brushed the tip of my tongue and I tried to lick it, but it pulled out of reach. When I sensed him bring it back, I stuck out my tongue to try to taste it but it retracted, teasing me. The next time he touched my tongue, I playfully nipped at his finger.

"You're so feisty," he murmured into my neck then bit the skin playfully, sparking a dangerous current of desire. I wanted to grab his hair and pull him in further but was aware I needed to follow his rules.

"That's because you're teasing me."

"Am I? Tell me what you want," he purred against my neck.

"I want to taste it in my mouth."

"What do you want to taste?"

"You know what."

"Tell me."

"Your finger."

"Good." He slowly moved his finger into my mouth and I swirled my tongue around it. "That's it. Just like that."

His voice was oozing with desire, which only increased the growing ache in my sex.

"Are you focusing on just the sensations in your mouth?" he asked, his tongue making slow, sensual licks along the throbbing vein in my neck while his finger was still in my mouth.

"Mmhmm," I lied.

His breathing was as labored as mine. Suddenly, his lips and finger pulled away and I began to think I had done something wrong. Then his mouth was on mine. I parted my lips for him and his tongue slipped inside, the tip tasting of rich, creamy dark chocolate. The taste of his mouth mixed with chocolate was overwhelmingly sensual. I reached up and ran my hands through his silky hair, grabbing and pulling his mouth deeper into mine, all resistance and restraint gone. I didn't care for his rules anymore. I wanted him so badly it was physically painful.

"No hands," he grunted, soft lips becoming rough. I could tell he was trying to act upset because I'd broken his rule and the thin veil masking his desire only intensified my yearning for him.

Suddenly, he wrapped one arm around my torso and the other behind my knees. He lifted me into the air like a bride, mouth never leaving mine. We must've entered his bedroom because the next thing I knew, silk sheets hit my back. Hot with need, I parted my legs to accommodate his hips pushing between them.

My hands tightened, craving the feel of the hard muscles of his back. His hips against mine, I felt the solid weight of his erection through his pants press against my stomach.

"You feel that? That's how much I want you."

"I feel it." My voice trembled with desire sensing what was coming.

He ground his erection against my sex in slow, firm circles. Even through the layers of our clothes, the pressure and friction sent currents of pleasure, fueling my hunger for direct contact. "Tell me what you want," he whispered hoarsely.

"I want to feel you inside me, Vincent."

He grabbed both of my hands and raised my arms over my head, pinning them with one firm hand while the other skillfully unbuttoned my jeans. "Keep your arms here, Kristen. Otherwise I won't let you have it. Understand?" Only a slight waver in his tone betrayed the steely control he projected.

"I want to feel you though. I want to see you," I protested, not understanding why he was torturing me with desperate need. He'd wanted this ever since our first meeting and now that he had me dripping with desire, he was taking his sweet time. I needed him inside me. Now.

"Nothing worth pursuing comes without patience," he said, throwing my own words back at me, inciting frustration that only intensified my arousal. His tone softened. "Clench the pillow behind your head if you need to. I promise, this will be worth it."

I grumbled approval, so horny I was afraid I was losing my mind.

I wiggled my hips to aid him as he gracefully slipped off my jeans along with my panties. A moment later, I heard them thud in a faraway corner. "God, Kristen. Your cunt is so beautiful."

His filthy words sent fresh juices to my aching sex. I crossed my legs, embarrassed of what he might see. Although I'd shaved recently, I was self-conscious about him viewing such a vulnerable area of my body.

He parted my legs with firm hands. "Don't hide such a beautiful thing from me. I want to see it. I want to see everything. Show me."

I'd always been a little shy being nude in front of a man, but compelled by the urgency in his tone, I did as he asked. Somehow he had the ability to make me feel beautiful.

Then I felt something slowly enter me. A finger.

"So wet. So soft. *Damn it*." He growled, as if straining to hold back a primal desire threatening to consume him. His mouth was close to my pussy, his hot labored breaths brushing my clit. I imagined him staring at me, dark eyes inflamed with lust, watching as he pushed his finger into my eagerly awaiting slit. If only I didn't have this blindfold on, I could see his gorgeous face.

He thrust his finger in up to the second knuckle, and I bit my lip, trying to hold back the moan building inside my throat. It'd been so long since I'd been touched, I was afraid I'd come from that single motion alone.

"You're already close aren't you?"

I nodded painfully, fingers desperately clutching the pillow, perspiration misting my skin.

His finger resumed thrusting in and out, twisting as it did so. First slowly, then faster. His pace increased edging me closer to my impending climax.

"Oh my god, I'm coming."

The orgasm slammed into me, shattering my senses. I arched into his hand and my sex clenched his finger.

Before I could fully recover, I felt sensation against my clit.

"No, Vincent. I'm too sensitive."

His expert tongue lapped hungrily at the hood, periodically dipping into my cleft and nuzzling my clit with his nose. After my mind-blowing orgasm, I didn't think my body could take anymore.

"So good. So sweet." He groaned as he devoured me, sending my head spinning. I writhed on the bed and released my grip from the pillow behind me. I reached for luscious locks, pulling his tongue deeper into my cleft as I bucked my hips. I'd never experienced such brain-sizzling oral pleasure before.

"It feels too good," I moaned.

"I've never been this hard before," he growled. "I want you so bad."

"Take me," I cried.

His head moved away and I heard buttons scatter as he ripped his shirt. His belt buckle and pants soon followed. I knew he freed his cock because there was a dull skin-slapping sound as it hit my stomach. I reached to touch it, to feel its scorching heat and pulsing energy. It was heavy and long enough to accommodate both my hands.

"You don't know how much I've thought about those hands wrapping around my cock." His voice was desperate and needy. I squeezed him and he released a pained cry.

"Can I take the blindfold off?" I pleaded.

"Yes. Take it off. Everything off."

With one hand, I pulled away the folded napkin and I gazed at what was in my other hand.

"Jesus, you're big."

My gaze snagged on the hard tapered lines of his pelvis. And ripped. My gaze trailed from his hips up and across steely abs and chiseled pecs pierced with silver rings to his breathtaking face, dark eyes flushed with desire. I'd seen him in his swimsuit before, but now he was completely nude, radiating raw sexual energy that stole my breath.

"I can't fight it anymore, Kristen. I need to be inside you."

He reached into a bedside drawer and produced a small packet. I released my grip as he roughly took his member in his own hands and wrapped himself before guiding it to my entrance. I sucked in a deep breath preparing for his size. Although I used a vibrator, Vincent looked bigger than what I was used to. I anticipated he'd impatiently thrust to the hilt, but he took his time, slowly parting the folds with the head. With how wet I was, he was easily able to slide in. He stopped when the tip was fully inside and pulled back with the same patience, slowly stroking my walls with just the head, cycling sensations of emptiness and fullness again and again. The teasing was agonizing.

"Deeper," I begged.

He pushed deeper, unhurried, every ridge of his heated flesh firing nerves I didn't realize I had. My mind swam in the experience.

"Faster," I panted.

"You said slow."

I began to regret having said those words to him during our date in St. Thomas, but then his pace quickened. I gripped his backside and pulled, aiding his thrusts as I bucked forward for stronger penetration. It'd been so long since I had sex that the pleasure from Vincent moving inside me was almost unbearable. Consumed by desire, our mouths and bodies wrestled in primal lust, cries of pleasure echoing throughout the apartment.

"You're making me lose it, Kristen. I can't stop."

His thrusts became more urgent, more desperate as did my moans. Then I felt him jerk and the first wave of heat poured into me. He released a strangled growl the moment I clenched around him. He collapsed into me as my world went dark again for a moment. We laid there for a spell, neither of us speaking, just the sound of our heavy breaths and heartbeats filling the silence.

"You're incredible," Vincent said, lifting his face to look into my gaze.

I smiled, staring back into those dark eyes brimming with warm affection. "I was thinking the same thing."

"I thought I was going to die there for a moment."

"I'm not sure I haven't."

He smiled and kissed my cheek. "You're still here. With me."

Chapter Nine

We were standing among the impressive marble pillars of the library, looking out at the red brick buildings of Harvard Square. It was autumn and the red and yellow leaves fluttering down beneath the waning sun made a picturesque setting for a stupid argument about a post on my Facebook wall.

"Just tell me who he is!" the man yelled, his brown hair combed just above his bright blue eyes perfectly, as always. Together with his rimless glasses, he resembled a J Crew model.

"He's a friend from a class. It's nothing!"

It was the third time we'd fought that week. We were never a couple that fought a lot, but for some reason we'd been getting into more and more arguments recently. A year older, he'd graduated before me and gotten a job at his dad's law firm in Boston. Since then, he'd visited me regularly on campus, which I was grateful for, but knowing I was surrounded by other attractive guys my age seemed to make his jealousy worse.

He looked around. "You swear it's nothing?"

I hated having to deal with this part of our relationship. We'd been through this argument before—some guy waving at me or saying hello, sharing class notes, or asking if I wanted to go to a social event—and every time it ended with tears and hurt feelings. For both of us. It got to the point where we decided to share phone, email, and Facebook passwords.

"Oh my god, yes."

He took another look around and held out his hand, pinky extended. "Fine. Pinky swear."

Childish as it was, I was glad to be done with the argument. The past few months he'd been flipping out over every single guy who even looked at me, and it was a problem. I hoped I had at least avoided anything more extreme. But when I looked at his cold blue eyes, I was unsure. I glanced around sheepishly, but the campus was mostly deserted, finals having ended weeks ago.

I held out my pinky and intertwined it with his, hoping the action would appease him. His eyes flashed and he yanked me to his chest, twisting my finger savagely. I gasped, the full weight of the dread I had been carrying for weeks finally rising to the surface of my mind. As the pain erupted, hot tears flooded my eyes. My other hand shot up to pry my injured hand away from him, but he was too strong.

"Don't ever lie to me Kristen. Never. Do you understand me? Never."

My world blurred as tears poured down my cheeks. I tried desperately to scream for help but as I opened my mouth, his hand shot up to cover it. The world went gray.

I woke up screaming. A bundle of nerves, it didn't help I couldn't recognize my surroundings. Where was I?

"Kristen," a familiar voice said, "it was just a dream. You're okay."

I turned to Vincent beside me. His face was full of concern and his hand was wrapped gently around my shoulder. Realization swept over me. He was mostly right, it had been a dream. Not *just* a dream, but I was safe for now. I turned to him.

"That must have been a bad nightmare. Do you remember it?"

I remembered it in more ways than one. It had been the breaking point with Marty. Our relationship had seemed good for a long time, but when he started getting abusive it got ugly fast. That had been over two years ago.

"Vincent, I think—" I faltered. There was no need to unload this story on him right now. I barely knew him; I had been handling Marty on my own for two years without any issue, I could keep handling him for a while longer.

He pulled me tightly against his bare chest. The warmth and hardness was immediately comforting. "It's okay. Take a minute. You're safe here."

I traced my finger around one of his nipple rings. They were starting to grow on me. Again, he was right. I did need a minute because my heart was pounding. The more I thought about it, the more I couldn't believe Marty had actually shown up at my apartment.

He began stroking my hair down to my nape. Slowly I felt myself relaxing. Vincent was really being amazing about this. It would have been easy to wake me up and then roll over, dismissing my unease, but the way he was holding me close and comforting me was perfect.

"What was your nightmare about?" he asked.

I thought about telling him, but I just couldn't. It was too early in our relationship, or whatever it was we were doing. If I told him, he would probably feel like I was unloading way too much baggage way too quickly. He was already treating me differently than his other women. I didn't want to push it.

"Nothing," I said.

"You were thrashing around pretty hard for a dream about nothing."

"I just mean I don't remember."

He said nothing for a few minutes, continuing to stroke my hair. Finally, he spoke. "If you don't want to tell me, just say so, but please don't lie to me. I hate being lied to."

"Okay, fine, I don't want to tell you."

"Why?"

"Because this is our second date and things are already moving fast enough as it is."

"The more you build this up the more I want to know. I want to be close to you. I thought that's what you wanted. Not just casual dating and sex."

I said nothing, thinking. It was sweet that he wanted to be close to me, but this was just too soon. Maybe I could just make something up. It would be lying again, but at least this situation would be resolved.

"There's no point in obeying people's arbitrary rules about dating or anything else, really," he said. "You either feel safe with someone or you don't. It doesn't matter how long you've been together."

I took a deep breath. "You really think for yourself, don't you?"

"Telling people where to go with their arbitrary rules is one of the biggest reasons I am where I am." He pulled me in tighter. "Which, I might add, is a pretty amazing spot right now."

I smiled, but continued to say nothing. Could I really trust him not to run away when he found out about my past with Marty? He was saying all the right things, and I really didn't have a reason to believe he was lying, but it all seemed too good to be true. My cautious side was blaring for me to slow down.

And yet, I probably wasn't going to get a better chance to tell him about Marty than this moment. If he reacted badly, at least I would know that he was asking for me to tell him.

I pulled gently away. *Here we go.* "My ex-boyfriend showed up at my apartment today."

He scrunched his brow. "Does this have something to do with your dream?"

"It was about him."

He nodded, eyes still squinting. "So you still have feelings for him?"

I shuddered and he squeezed my shoulder. "No, no. Nothing like that. It's just—"

I faltered again. He looked at me, concern etched on his face. I started to cry and had to take several deep breaths to calm myself down enough to speak. "He was kind of abusive," I managed.

Vincent's mouth thinned to a tight line, and I saw his jaw working. He inhaled sharply, features shifting in a way I'd never seen before. Would he think I was weak or, worse, helpless because I had been abused?

"What do you mean, kind of?"

When I didn't say anything he shook his head, "It doesn't matter, where does he live?" His eyes were alight with violent promise.

"No—I mean—I don't know. Don't hurt him Vincent, it's not worth it."

"You let me decide whether it's worth it or not."

I started crying harder. This wasn't the reaction I was expecting. Vincent looked like he was ready to pound Marty's head in. It was sweet that he was feeling protective of me, but getting violent wasn't going to help anything. I hated violence.

When he saw me crying the hard lines in his face melted. He was breathing fast, but the fire in his eyes was mostly gone.

"I'm sorry. I didn't mean to upset you. What did he do to you, exactly?"

I shook my head. "Please don't make me go into details. I'm through with him and he can't hurt me anymore." How would I explain getting caught in a relationship with a man who had borderline personality disorder? How he was so sweet at first, and very attentive, but then would snap at a moment's notice? How he managed to hold it together for the outside world, but not with me? How it felt to beat yourself up over wanting to leave someone who had a legitimate mental illness they couldn't really help?

"Okay, okay. You're right. No need to dig up the past." He didn't say anything else, and I was grateful that he wasn't pressuring me any more about this even though I could tell questions were running through his mind.

I put my ear back down onto his chest and draped my arm over him. After a moment, he hugged me close, his hand resting on my hip. "I haven't spoken to him in years and somehow he knows where I live. It's unsettling."

"What happened when he came to your apartment?"

"Riley answered the door, and he told her he was looking for me. She texted me his description and I recognized it immediately. When I went to check on her I told her not to answer the door again."

"It sounds like he might be dangerous. You should stay here with me until we get this worked out. Or I can put you up in a hotel."

This was moving way too fast. I hadn't told him about this so he could fix the problem for me. "No, Vincent. I can't ask you to do that."

"You're not asking, I'm offering."

I said nothing.

He sighed. "Fine. No hotel then. I'll get you a security team. I know a couple of guys at Blackthorn Security, you'll barely notice them."

I shook my head.

"Think about it." He looked intensely at me for a moment before speaking again. "Can you go to the police?"

"I doubt it. They wouldn't do anything in Cambridge."

"Figures. They're never good for anything. What's his name?" When he saw the look on my face he continued, "I won't do anything to him, I promise."

I wouldn't have told him, but the solemn look on his face comforted me. Vincent wasn't the kind of guy who made promises lightly.

"Martin Pritchard. I called him Marty."

He nodded slowly. "Where did you meet him?"

"We dated all through college. He started out being really nice, but gradually got more and more possessive and jealous."

"Did he hurt you?"

"Please don't." I took a deep breath, trying to quell the nausea I had begun to feel as I recalled my dream.

Vincent said nothing and we sat in silence for a couple minutes. "Please let me get you a security team. You'll barely notice them, and they could save your life."

"Vincent, I told you this because you wanted to know, not so you could solve this problem for me. I can deal with my own issues." I was scared of Marty, but I really didn't want to seem weak in front of Vincent, like a woman who needed saving. What if I counted on him and then he disappeared? I would only have myself to blame.

His jaw was working again, but he didn't say anything for a minute. "Fine. Do you at least have some way to defend yourself if he tries to attack you? Mace, a knife, a gun, anything?"

My head spun at the thought of owning a deadly weapon. What kind of person did he think I was? "No. Why on earth would I own a gun?"

"Let's get you something tomorrow. Not a gun, but something."

I shrugged as hot tears began budding up in my eyes and running down my cheeks. He was listening, but he sounded very worried about this. I already regretted telling him. He wasn't running away, which was good, but I didn't want him to feel obligated, or like I was too weak to deal with this on my own.

Arm still around me, he rocked me onto my back so he was over me, brown eyes searching mine. "Kristen, I'm glad you told me about this. We can handle it however you want, okay?"

I nodded, though the tears were still coming thick. As the burden of the whole situation began to lift off my shoulders I realized how stressed I had been.

Vincent kissed away the tears rolling down my cheeks with soft little pecks. The way his muscles bulged as he cradled my head in his arms felt comforting. I really didn't want to deal with this right now.

"Let's forget about this for now," I said. "We can go to the store tomorrow like you suggested. I'd prefer not to think about it anymore tonight."

"Okay." He continued kissing away the tears on my face, sprinkling in kisses on my forehead.

I shifted and felt his cock through his underwear with my leg. Even when he wasn't hard, the size of his package was impressive.

He wasn't aroused, but I was getting to be. I needed a distraction from this situation. I had an idea of how I wanted to distract myself as I reached down to grab him through his underwear.

"I think I know how I want to handle this," I said.

He looked uncertain. "Are you sure? We can just go to sleep if you want."

"I don't. I want you inside me. I want my mind off this." I peeled his underwear down his legs and free of his feet. He didn't resist.

As soon as I had, he wrapped me up in his muscular arms and kissed me passionately on the lips, his hand moving down my torso to my panties as I stroked his cock. The way he responded so quickly to my touch heated my core.

"I can do that," he whispered into my ear, his hand hovering over my aching sex. "Let's take our time."

Our sex was slow and deeply passionate. Vincent kept himself close to me, cradling me chest to chest as he moved in and out. When we came together, it was the closest I had ever felt to another person. Afterwards, he took care of the condom and came back to scoop me up across his lap.

"That was incredible," he said.

"I agree. I'm exhausted." I was in a serious post-coital bliss, actually.

He took a deep breath. "Kristen," he said, "I will never let anyone hurt you."

It was touching that he was still thinking about the situation with Marty. "You don't have to protect me, Vincent."

"You're not asking me to, but I will."

I scooched up so my hand rested on his chest and looked into his earnest face. It was at that point that I realized that I really believed it when he said it. Maybe Vincent was my type after all. As I closed my eyes and snuggled closer into his embrace, the last image I saw was the light of my cell phone, the only light in the room. It burned for a second against the backs of my lids then slid away, leaving me to bask in the warmth of the moment.

Thank you for reading!

If you could spare a moment to leave a review it would be much appreciated.

Reviews help new readers find my books and decide if it's right for them. It also provides valuable feedback for my writing!

Sign up for my mailing list to find out when the next book the Surrender Series is released!

http://eepurl.com/sH7wn

2/2019 S

Made in the USA
Lexington, KY
23 January 2014